THREADS OF FATE (SPECIAL EDITION)

CHRONICLES OF THE SOVEREIGNS

BOOK ONE

LANA J WILLIAMS

BOOKS BY LANA J. WILLIAMS

<u>Chronicles of the Sovereigns</u>
Threads of Fate
The Mourner's Song (Prequel)
Threads of Betrayal

INTRODUCTION

Stories have always been how I make sense of the world. They are threads, sometimes tangled things that tie us to one another and to the mysteries beyond what we can see. Threads of Fate was born out of my own wonder about balance. How can love feel like rebellion? How can grief and joy coexist? And how is peace both fragile and ferocious?

This book is the beginning of a much larger tapestry. The Sovereigns are not just gods in some faraway realm. To me, they are reflections of our strengths, our failings, our longings. Eira's story is one of defiance and tenderness, of breaking rules for the sake of something greater than fear.

If you are holding this book, I want to thank you. For stepping into a world that has lived in my heart, for lending your imagination to these characters and for daring to walk through the veil with me.

THE SOVEREIGNS

A list of The Sovereigns and their pronunciations.

1. Life – Zivael (*ZEE-vayl*)

2. Death – Thaloré (*THA-lor-ay*)

3. Mercy – Elestra (*eh-LESS-truh*)

4. Revenge – Vireth (*VEER-eth*)

5. Pleasure – Sedara (*seh-DAHR-uh*)

6. Pain – Akria (*ACK-ree-uh*)

7. Fury – Thamys (*THAH-miss*)

8. Peace – Eira (*AY-rah*)

9. Joy – Lysera (*lih-SAIR-uh*)

10. Sorrow – Melora (*meh-LOR-uh*)

PROLOGUE

In the beginning, there was silence. From that silence came the Loom, and it was vast, eternal and omnipotent. It wove the first threads of existence that became light and shadow, creation and ending, the rise and fall of every heartbeat yet to come. Its patterns were law. Its cuts, final.

But from the Loom's threads rose ten Sovereigns, each born of a truth the world could not live without. Life to give breath. Death to take it. Mercy to forgive. Revenge to punish. Pleasure to tempt. Pain to teach. Fury to burn. Peace to soothe. Joy to brighten. Sorrow to mourn.

Together they became the Pantheon guardians. Bound by the Loom's Law, they could only watch, whisper, and wait. Never could they shape a mortal's will. And above all, they could never love a mortal. For love changes fate, and fate was meant to be unchanging. Yet the threads tremble. Balance frays. A choice approaches that even the Sovereigns fear to name. And it begins not with gods, but a single mortal man.

PART ONE

The Unraveling

CHAPTER I

EIRA

Rain softened the city into blurred strokes of gray and light. Neon signs bled down the slick streets, their reflections stretching across puddles like veins of fire and wine. Tires hissed on wet asphalt, umbrellas bobbed past the windows, and the faint hum of life outside pressed faintly against the glass walls of the coffee shop at the corner of Seventh and Willow.

Inside, the world felt warmer, steadier. The bitter-sweet aroma of roasted beans lingered in the air, mingling with cinnamon and chocolate, with the earthy heat of steamed milk. A soft jazz track drifted through the speakers, barely audible above the chatter of students bent over laptops, tired office workers cradling mugs, and couples speaking in hushed tones.

Eira sat in the farthest booth, her figure cloaked in a pale gray coat, her hood pulled low. Mortals seldom noticed her as the veil she wore in this realm muted what she truly was, softened the edges of her divinity.

To them, she looked like any other woman. Perhaps a little too still, perhaps a little too pale, her eyes too sharp when caught in the light. But mortals rarely looked long enough to see the difference.

Her gaze, calm and unblinking, rested on the flatscreen bolted above the counter. Bold red letters crawled across the bottom of the screen:

Breaking News: New World Government Votes to Ban Paper Currency

The feed cut to footage of streets crowded with protesters. Anger surged in the air, visible through the screen showing hundreds of people with raised fists and contorted faces, their banners snapping in the wind.

Riot police held their lines, shields gleaming in the rain. Someone shouted into a megaphone, their voice drowned by the roar of the crowd.

Eira pressed her hand lightly to her chest, inhaling deeply. She did not need the broadcast to tell her what she already felt. The tremor of unrest was woven through her domain, gnawing at the seams of her essence. Peace had been fracturing for centuries, but this felt different. This was not the restless turbulence of human politics. This was imbalance.

Her siblings would not be surprised. She had warned them long ago that the Balance was tipping. They had listened politely, some even with a trace of pity, but none had taken her warning to heart. Fury had laughed at her unease. Revenge had smirked, his silence sharp as a blade. Joy had danced past the topic with a smile as was her nature, Mercy had shaken her head in sorrow, and even Sorrow herself had only bowed her head as if she already knew what was to come.

They thought her role was simple, perhaps even unnecessary. Peace, the still one, the quiet one, the soft one. She was not fire like Fury, not blood like Pain, not intoxicating as Pleasure or terrifying as Death. But without her, the threads frayed. She had always known this, and lately she had begun to wonder if she alone remembered. Her thoughts drifted as the rain traced crooked rivers down the glass. She watched the storm because it was easier than watching the news, the heaviness of it weighing on her heart like an anchor. It was easier than admitting that she could feel her own weakness gnawing at her.

Movement caught her eye, causing her to turn her head a fraction. Not the flicker of the screen this time, but the rapid motion of a pen scratching against paper. Her gaze drifted to the man across the shop. She hadn't noticed him before, but how could she not? She was always watching, always vigilant. He was not like the others hunched over laptops or glowing screens, not dulled by the grayness of long days. He was...striking.

Dark, wavy hair fell to his shoulders, damp at the ends as though the rain itself had followed him inside. His skin carried the warmth of sunlight, golden even beneath the cafe's dim lights, as though touched by some place the storms could not reach. His face was carved with symmetry mortals rarely held, cheekbones sharp as blades, a strong jaw that caught the light when he tilted his head. But it was his eyes that held her: dark pools, fathomless, like midnight waters with no stars to soften them.

He had the look of a man sculpted for myth rather than this gray city. His body spoke of strength, hard muscle shifting easily beneath the plain clothes he wore, though there was no vanity in his posture. He carried himself as one who had never realized how the world might look at him, as though unaware of his own gravity. Other mortals glanced at him occasionally, eyes lingering before sliding away, unsettled by something they couldn't name. Eira knew what it was. Beauty such as his felt too much like divinity. Too much like her own kind. And yet, here he sat, surrounded by a chaos of napkins, his tawny skin smudged with ink.

At first, Eira thought nothing of it. Mortals drew endlessly, chasing meaning they rarely grasped. She had been more captivated by his stunning features than his focused scribbling. But then one napkin tilted toward the light, and she saw. They weren't doodles. Her breath caught in her throat. Black lines curved and wove in familiar shapes and spirals, echoing the very patterns she had guarded since before the first star was born. Threads. They weren't literal but they were somehow unmistakable. What Eira saw was the weave of fate, the strands of inevitability, and the very essence that kept the balance of all living things.

Eira's fingers tightened around her untouched mug. Mortals could not see such things, should not be able to draw them to perfection like this man had. Not unless they were marked, cursed, or... her thoughts strayed to hundreds of infinite possibilities, all the more frightening for the man. He tore the napkin and began his frantic scribbling again. Another spiral, another weave, another fracture. And then she saw it clearly: a thread splitting, jagged and raw. Her pulse, steady as still water for centuries, quickened. She leaned forward, compelled, though she knew she should not. He was nothing to her. This man was a mortal. Fragile, fleeting, bound by time. She was the opposite- eternal, everlasting, her essence extending beyond time. And yet he sketched with the desperation of someone tracing truth with bare hands, a truth that he should know nothing of.

The napkin slipped from his fingers and drifted to the floor. Eira rose before she could stop herself. Her movements were soundless, her presence hushed. She crossed the shop, stooping to lift the napkin while staring at what should be an impossibility etched on it. Ink stained its surface, revealing two threads breaking apart violently, left dangling and incomplete.

She stared at it too long. Then, softly, words slipped from her lips. "You see it."

Her eyes bore into him, and she felt something snap within herself. A strange, unusual feeling. Whether he noticed it or not, she felt it, whatever it was. The man looked up, his expression startled. His head lifted and his eyes, dark pools of midnight, locked onto hers. Most mortals, when caught in her gaze, flinched or turned away. But he did not. He met her stare head-on, steady and unafraid.

"See what?" He replied, his voice warm like a summer day and a rich glass of whiskey. He looked her up and down and his brows scrunched, as if trying to picture where he knew her from.

"This," she said, tilting the napkin toward him.

Recognition flickered in his face, swift and undeniable. His hand hovered above the scattered sketches as if caught between snatching them away and showing her more.

"You...see it too?" he asked, low, cautious, but tinged with something like relief. His eyebrows knit together as he waited for her answer. Eira froze. The right answer, which was probably the safest answer, was no. She should have returned the napkin, smiled politely, and left. But his eyes held hers as though he had been waiting all his life for her answer.

"I thought I was the only one," he continued before she could reply. His gaze dropped to the mess of ink and paper. "People laugh. They think I'm eccentric or broken. A drunk, perhaps. I honestly can't explain it- it just happens. If I don't draw them, I feel like I'll come apart."

Eira's chest ached with recognition. She knew that sensation all too well. What he described was the weight of inevitability pressing so hard that to ignore it was to fracture. She had lived it for millennia.

"What do you call it?" she asked.

A crooked smile tugged at his lips. "Nothing. They're just... threads. I've always called them that."

The word struck her like a bell tolling in the distance. She hesitated, then gestured faintly to the chair across from him. "May I?"

He blinked, surprised, then nodded. "Sure. I'm Adrian, by the way."

"Eira," she said, her voice soft and melodic.

The name lingered between them. He tilted his head, tasting the sound. "That's...unique. So is your accent. You aren't from around here, are you?" He smiled warmly, flashing a set of brilliantly white teeth.

Remembering that she needed to make human- like gestures, she shrugged, looking back down at the mess of napkins.

"No, I'm not from around here. I only come here to visit on occasion." she smiled, a genuine one, before continuing. "And yes, my name is rather- special. I guess I should say I was raised with very... old fashioned parents. You could even call them ancient." She suppressed a smirk at that last part. It was true- just not in the way mortals would interpret it.

Silence fell, but it was not uncomfortable. Adrian shifted, self-conscious about the chaos of napkins littering his table. His eyes flitted around the table before locking eyes with her once more.

"Most of these don't make sense. Half the time I don't even know what I'm drawing. It's like I'm copying something I've already seen, but I can't remember where or when." He gave a short, nervous laugh. "I sound insane, don't I?"

Eira studied him, her eyes unreadable. "No," she said slowly, "You sound...like you're listening to what the universe is telling you. I think we all should be listening a lot more these days."

His gaze lifted at that, wary but searching, as though she had struck closer to truth than she should have. Around them, the coffee shop hummed on with the hustle and bustle of everyday life. Mortals came and went, baristas called names, mugs clinked. Yet for Eira, the room had narrowed to this table, this mortal, and the sketches that should not exist. And as she sat there, Balance stirred. The lights flickered. Somewhere near the counter, a glass trembled, rolled, and shattered against the floor.

Eira's fingers curled around the napkin in her hand. She should leave now. She should walk away before the world demanded consequence. But Adrian was still watching her. And for the first time in centuries, she could not convince her feet to move.

CHAPTER 2
EIRA

The storm had thickened by the time Eira left the coffee shop. Rain slashed across the streets as it poured from the sky, blurring the city in a haze of light and shadow. Wind pressed against her hood, carrying the smell of wet asphalt and electricity. Above her, thunder rolled low, steady as the beat of a war drum.

She felt it before she stepped fully into the street. Balance. It was not a voice, not a presence she could name, but a force pressing at the edges of her being. The warning was unmistakable. She had lingered too long and meddled too much. She had been seen, and possibly felt. Already, the world was shifting to remind her of the Law she had brushed against. The Law which, she knew, was never to be broken.

Her hand tightened around the napkin still folded in her pocket. Adrian's sketch burned against her like a brand. Threads fractured, jagged, incomplete. She had felt that break long before tonight, but in his hands, the vision was too precise to ignore. She should leave now. Disappear into the veil, return to her realm before Balance struck harder. It was the only safe choice.

"Eira?" a male voice called after her.

Her name carried softly through the rain, and she froze. She stood there for a minute, too still.

Unearthly still. And slowly, she turned to face the mortal man who had stopped her heart for a fraction of a second.

He stood beneath the awning of the coffee shop, his sketchbook clutched against his side. The warm glow of the shop spilled across him, painting his skin in warm light against the storm. His hair clung to his shoulders where the rain had caught him, and his eyes- those dark, fathomless pools- fixed on her with a mix of disbelief and longing.

For the briefest moment, she could not move. He should not have followed her. He should have let her vanish back into anonymity, forgotten as all mortals were meant to forget. She wished she could make him forget, but she knew instinctively that using that gift could cost him. It could possibly cost her. He stepped forward into the storm, as though he couldn't help himself. He moved closer to her, appearing to be in some sort of a daze. For a moment, Eira wondered if her mere presence had affected him, had lured him toward her. She didn't have to wonder for long.

"Wait," Adrian said, voice raised over the wind. "Please. Don't go yet."

The pressure in her chest deepened. Balance trembled harder, the storm surging in answer.

"Go back inside," she told him, her voice sharper than she intended. "It isn't safe for you out here. This weather is terrible."

Adrian shook his head, rain plastering his hair to his temples. "I don't care. I need to-"

The screech of tires tore through the night.

Eira's head snapped toward the sound. A car, skidding across the slick pavement, its headlights slicing through the rain, hurtled toward the curb. Toward Adrian. He froze, wide-eyed like a deer caught in headlights. There was no time for him to react, no time to do much of anything. Time stretched, thin and brittle until Eira could almost feel it snap. She decided right then, balance be damned, what her choice would be.

Eira moved, swift and silent like the rustle of wind through leaves. In less than a heartbeat she was there, her hand closing around his arm. With a force no mortal should possess, she yanked him back, her body slamming against his as the car screamed past, close enough that the wind tore at their clothes. Water sprayed in its wake, the horn blaring before it vanished into the storm.

Silence followed, punctuated only by the gentle patter of rain. Adrian's breath came in ragged gasps against her ear. She was still holding him, her hand locked around his arm, her body pressed against his in a shield. For a moment she forgot to let go. For a moment...she didn't want to. It *felt* right, their bodies pressed together like this. But Eira knew that she was treading the delicate line that would be breaking sacred Law.

When she released Adrian he staggered back, staring at her as though the world had split open. His eyes widened as they swept over her face, her hands, her posture and she knew what he saw. He saw *her*. Not the mortal veil she wore to dampen the divinity radiating from her very existence. He didn't see her entirely, though. In her divine form, he might not survive the sight.

In the lightning's flash, her skin glowed faintly, her eyes gleamed too steady, too bright.

"What-" His voice broke. He swallowed hard, rain slicking his bronze skin, dark hair clinging to his cheek. "What-what are you? What was that?" The words poured from his lips like an accusation and struck her like a blade. Eira turned away sharply and pulled her hood lower, attempting to tuck a few strands of her auburn hair away.

"Forget what you saw," she said as she walked away swiftly,

cursing herself for intervening with Fate's plans. This blatant act of disrespect, she knew, would have consequences. Who was she to interfere with mortal business and things that were fated to occur? She was not the Architect. She held no power over the grand design.

"Don't ever speak of this, to anyone." She called over her shoulder, hastening her stride. "Ever."

"Forget?" Adrian let out a short, breathless laugh, half disbelief with a twinge of hysteria. "You pulled me like I weighed nothing. You-your eyes-" He quickened his pace to match hers, moving closer, lowering his voice but not his intensity. "You're not like anyone I've ever met. I don't even know you, but I feel like I do." He placed a hand across his heart as he spilled this confession.

She forced herself to stay still, though her pulse hammered. The Law was clear: no Sovereign may reveal themselves to a mortal in their divine form. To do so risked unraveling everything. Did that really matter, though, when he had seen a glimpse of her true being without her removing her glamour?

The question lingered in Eira's mind, but she knew the truth. She felt it. Balance had already felt the fracture, and this man-this beautiful, cursed man-was already too deep.

"You shouldn't be near me," she said, her voice low, meant to cut. "It's dangerous for you. It could ruin everything!" she hissed the last part, clearing her throat to regain control.

His jaw tightened. Rain traced the lines of his face, glistening on his lashes, his lips. "Then why does it feel like I've been waiting for you?"

The words stole her breath. She stared at him, unable to look away, the world narrowing again to the space between them. She saw the stubborn set of his jaw, the flicker of defiance in his dark eyes, the raw honesty that mortals carried without shame. And for a heartbeat, she almost believed him. The storm answered for her. Lightning tore across the sky, thunder cracking hard enough to rattle windows. Eira flinched, something she did not do often. Balance was screaming now.

She stepped back, shaking her head. "Don't follow me again, Adrian."

Adrian shook his head, his voice rough with desperation. "I can't just let this go. You saw what I drew. You knew it. You're the first person who hasn't called me insane." He took another step toward her, rain streaming down his face. "You've got to give me something. You know what- fine, don't. Don't give me anything. But don't tell me to forget you."

Her hand tightened around the napkin crumpled in her pocket. There was no denying the pull from his art or from him. Even now, she could feel the sketch of broken threads pulsing against her like a heartbeat. But she knew it was safer to leave. Especially now that he had seen her. A chill ran up her spine and she could practically feel the vibration from Balance and knew there would be inconceivable consequences.

"Adrian," she said softly, the sound of his name strange on her tongue. For a moment she let herself linger there, let him see her eyes beneath the hood, unguarded. She let him glimpse the divinity that lurked beneath the surface. He inhaled sharply. She turned away before she could stop herself.

"Go home. Stay alive. That's all you need to do." Her voice was low, edged with a warning she didn't need to speak aloud. With that she stepped into the storm, the rain swallowing her figure until she vanished into the night.

Behind her, Adrian stood motionless in the downpour, the thunder cracking overhead. His chest heaved, his pulse still racing, his mind a riot of disbelief. In his hand, his sketchbook hung loose, pages curling from the rain. When he looked down, the ink had blurred, but one image remained sharp through the water. A woman cloaked in light, standing in the heart of a storm. Her eyes were his undoing. Her eyes, so normal but not. Her entire being- human, but other. He could feel it. Adrian closed the book slowly, his fingers trembling.

"I didn't imagine you," he whispered into the rain. But Balance had already heard.

CHAPTER 3
EIRA

The veil parted with a sigh as Eira stepped into her realm. The mortal storm vanished behind her. No flashing neon, no pounding rain, no protests shaking the streets. Here there was only endless water, still as glass, stretching into horizons that had no end. The sky was always dawn in her realm. The soft silver, pale gold light promised a morning it would never deliver.

Willows rose from the water's surface in graceful arcs, their long silver branches brushing like fingers across the mirrored plane. Every detail was hushed, eternal, serene. This was Peace. Her gift. Her burden. Her prison. And it was trembling.

Eira stopped walking and looked down. The water beneath her bare feet rippled without wind. Darkness bled faintly through the glassy surface, threads of shadow sliding like ink through clear water. Above her, the horizon quivered faintly, as though the sky itself breathed too quickly. Her heart sank. Even here, in her sanctuary, she could not keep the stillness.

She closed her eyes and drew in a deep, steady breath. Her presence alone should have been enough to calm the realm. For millennia it had been this way, her serenity spreading outward, restoring balance. The waters would smooth, the willows would bow in tranquil rhythm, the air would steady itself. But tonight, her breath faltered. Tonight, the cracks only widened. She pressed a hand against her chest as she thought about *him*. Adrian.

His face rose unbidden in her mind, disrupting her thoughts. She could vividly picture the dark waves of his hair clinging to his temples, his golden skin gleaming wet with rain, his eyes deep as midnight waters. Mortal. Fragile. Doomed to die. Yet she had touched him, pulled him from death's path, and revealed more of herself than she should have. And she had felt something stir. Something that was forbidden to her, and that terrified her.

The Law had been clear for eons: no Sovereign may love a mortal. To love was to alter fate. To love was to invite ruin. And yet... her chest tightened at the memory of him, at the mere thought of his name on her lips.

"You're rattled."

The words coming from the familiar voice cracked the stillness like fire through dry wood. Eira turned sharply. Across her mirrored waters a shadowy figure advanced, heavy steps rippling the surface with heat. Her brother, Fury, had come.

Thamys towered, broad-shouldered, his presence rolling like thunder. His hair hung in dark waves like smoke, his eyes molten gold, embers glowing in their depths. He wore the scent of ash and blood, the iron tang of battlefields. Heat shimmered around him, distorting the air. Where his boots struck her waters, steam rose, clashing with her cool mist. A grin stretched across his face that was too sharp to be kind, too fierce to be called joy.

"Strange," he said, sweeping a hand across her trembling horizon. "Your realm quivers. Your waters ripple. Peace, undone in her own domain. What rattles you, sister?"

"Leave," Eira said softly, though her voice was sharp. "This is not your domain and you have come uninvited."

"Ah, but Balance shouted." He took another step closer, the

mirrored water hissing under his feet. "When Balance roars, we all feel it. And the roar came from here. From you."

"I told you, Thamys-" Eira started but Fury cut her off with a laugh, booming and terrible.

"You broke the stillness. You, the perfect one. Admit it. Something troubles you. Or-" his eyes gleamed with mockery as his gaze swept over her- "someone."

Before she could answer, the air shifted. A new presence drifted in, cool and mournful, carrying the scent of lilies and rain-soaked stone. The mirrored water darkened in her wake, but not with heat. With sorrow.

"*Enough*, Fury," came a soft feminine voice. "You shake her realm more than she does herself."

Eira turned and found Melora gliding toward them. Sorrow was wrapped in deep indigo robes that trailed like ink bleeding into water. Her hair, black streaked with silver, floated in an unseen current. Her pale face bore the beauty of grief eternal, and her eyes, dark and endless, carried sorrow so profound it pressed against the heart. Melora's bare feet kissed the water silently. Where she passed, the willows bowed lower, as though mourning in her presence.

"Peace falters," Melora whispered, "And so the Balance falters too. What bothers you, dear sister?"

Eira closed her eyes. "You should not be here, Melora."

"Nor should you falter," Melora replied, gently. Fury barked a laugh. "Do not soften her fault, sister. She has broken the Law. Balance screamed because of her. I will not leave until she admits it."

Eira's voice was cold. "I owe you no confession. And have you forgotten so easily brother, that I can banish you from my realm?" A slight smirk teased the corners of her lips. "You'll get no confession from me."

Fury hissed, narrowing his eyes on her. "Then you leave me to make my own assumptions," he said, his grin sharp as a knife. "And I say you've tangled yourself with a *mortal*."

The word rang through the waters like a stone dropped in a well. Even Melora's gaze sharpened, sorrow deepening in her eyes. Eira's hands trembled at her sides. She tried to speak, to deny, but the words refused to form. Melora's voice was soft but cutting.

"Tell us the truth. Why does your realm tremble? Why did Balance roar?" Fury whispered, narrowing his gaze on Eira. "You know your defiance will cost you."

Eira lowered her head, absorbing the truth of his statement. Her auburn hair spilled like pale silk across her shoulders, shadowing her face. At last, in a whisper, she said, "Because he was going to die. And I am drawn to him, for reasons I do not yet understand."

The stillness shattered. The mirrored water beneath them rippled violently, waves spreading outward. Fury's laughter roared, cruel and booming. "So it's true! Peace, savior of mortals. Our sister breaks eternity's oldest law for a man of flesh and bone." He spat the last words, disgust written all across his beautiful face.

Melora's lips parted, her sorrow twisting into shock. "Eira... mortals die every day. It is their fate. Even Life yields them to Death without protest. You have watched countless pass without lifting a hand. Why him?"

Eira raised her head, her eyes glimmering like storms beneath still water. "Because he saw." Silence followed. Even Fury's grin faltered.

Melora's voice fell to a whisper. "Saw what, exactly? Sister, what do you mean to say?"

"The threads." Eira said, her voice low and steady. She was ashamed, but she would not back down. Not to her siblings, not to anyone.

Fury's grin returned, but colder. "Impossible. No mortal sees the Loom."

"He does," Eira insisted, her voice trembling with intensity. "He has seen them for years. He sketches them exactly as they are- spirals, fractures, woven patterns. When I looked upon his drawings, it was like gazing into the Loom itself." She pressed a hand against her chest. "He sees, though he cannot name it. He is not like the others."

Fury snarled a terrifying sound, the air sparking around him. "And so you risk eternity because a *mortal* scratches lines on paper? How pathetic." He spat the word mortal as if it were a curse, face contorted in disgust.

"They are not scratches!" Eira snapped. Her voice echoed like a bell through her realm, cracking the stillness. The waters rippled violently, silver leaves whipping in unseen wind. "They are truth, and they are Fate. He is touched by the threads. Balance led me to him. I know it."

Melora's face was stricken with grief, her sorrow deepening until it weighed on every word. "Sister... Balance does not lead. Balance only corrects. If he sees what he should not, then he is a fracture. And fractures are mended, not preserved."

Fury leaned closer, his heat searing against her cool air. "You broke the Law for him. Admit it. You revealed yourself. You saved him. What comes next, Eira? Will you love him? Will you fall for him, and in falling, doom him and the fate of this very universe?"

Eira's lips parted, but no sound came. For a heartbeat, her silence was answer enough. Fury's laughter roared again. "Then you are lost. We cannot help you, sister."

Melora stepped forward, her sorrow radiating like frost. "Do not mock her, Fury. This is no jest. If she continues, Balance will not punish her alone. It will punish him. Innocence means nothing to Balance."

Eira's chest ached and she closed her eyes, rubbing her temples. "I know."

"Then let him go," Melora whispered, her voice like a dirge. "Do not look for him again. Let him live his brief life and pass as all mortals do. Only then will the Balance steady."

Eira said nothing, and her silence was louder than denial. Fury spat into the water, and the hiss of steam curled like a serpent between them. "You are a fool. I will not hide your fault from the others. At the next Convergence, they will know. And they will not be merciful." With that, Fury turned, the air bending to his heat. He strode forward until the veil swallowed him whole.

Melora lingered, her eyes heavy with sorrow. She reached out, though her fingers never touched. "If you love him, sister, he will be the one to pay." Then she too was gone.

Silence returned, but it was not peace. Eira sank to her knees on the mirrored water, her reflection fractured beneath her. She pressed her trembling hands into her lap, her heart burning with both dread and longing. For the first time in eternity, she admitted a frightening truth to herself. She did not want to let Adrian go. Even if it destroyed her.

CHAPTER 4
ADRIAN

Sleep didn't come that night. Instead, it hovered out of reach like a word on the tip of his tongue. Adrian lay on his back and watched the ceiling glow and dim with each roll of lightning, the storm pacing the length of the city as if it were counting. When he closed his eyes to chase it, he found her instead. Eira.

He tried to give the name less power. He whispered it once, quietly, and it rang through him as if the room itself had bones that could carry sound. The name almost sounded foreign on his tongue, as if he shouldn't be speaking her name at all. He turned on his side and pulled the thin blanket higher, then gave up pretending, pushed himself upright, and swung his feet to the floor. Cold wood met the pads of his toes, and the jolt of it steadied him enough to breathe.

He'd had nights like this since childhood.

Nights when sleep refused him and something in the dark drew tight, turning his thoughts into a braid he couldn't untangle. He would sit up, take a pencil in his hand, and the world would pour through him in lines he didn't choose. His mother used to joke that he was born with ink under his nails; later, when the drawings turned strange, she stopped joking. She would stand in the doorway, the hall light making a halo around her hair, and she would ask if he was all right without stepping inside.

"I'm just drawing," he'd say, to avoid explaining himself.

"What is it this time?" his mother would ask, curiously.

"Patterns," would be his usual reply, because there wasn't a better word for what his hands could create.

He thought of those old pages sometimes- the early ones, messy and chaotic like the doodles of a child. Teachers had called them spiderwebs. A school counselor described them kindly as "compulsions," and suggested he channel them into something productive.

He took the suggestion seriously. Adrian learned how to shade, how to pull dimension from flat paper, and how to make shadows work like gravity. He added figures, faces and hands, then tried to stitch the patterns behind something people would recognize, as if disguising them would make them easier to carry. But wherever he put his pencil down, the lines found each other. They curved and crossed, split and returned. *Threads*. He'd hated the word for years but when he finally said it aloud to himself, the relief of honesty made him dizzy and sick.

There had been moments when other people almost saw. An art teacher in high school with ink- stained fingers and a voice like a saxophone had stood over his shoulder and gone quiet. "There's a... structure." she'd said, like a person spotting a constellation she didn't know she'd been missing. He remembered her hand hovering as if she might touch the page but thought better of it, as if it might be hot. "Don't be ashamed of this," she told him, and for a while he wasn't.

Then came the gallery years. Those stupid, hungry years when he learned to carry a portfolio and wear a jacket that didn't fit right and say things he only half believed. He spoke about negative space and palimpsest and the way cities make people braid their lives into each other. He watched faces as he talked, the way eyes lit or went blank. The ones who lit up never commissioned anything. The ones who went blank said "interesting," like a verdict.

Once, a woman named Mara who ran a white, bright space with nothing on the walls took a stack of his napkins and asked if she could keep them for a few days. When he said yes, his hands shook so hard he had to pretend he'd spilled coffee. He slept for the first time in a week after that and when he woke, he felt light.

Two days later, Mara gave the napkins back in a clear plastic sleeve. "They bother me," she'd said, and because she meant it-because the honesty had cost her enough to make her cheeks flush-he didn't hate her for it. He only hated himself for being so strange, and drawing things that made sense to no one, not even himself.

He had told himself that there were worse fates than being an artist nobody wanted. He could teach. He could do portraits in parks if he wanted to lean into romance and irony. He could keep drawing in private and be a person the rest of the time. He had friends who were good at that. But it always felt like trying to suffocate a part of himself. Then tonight, she had put a name to the thing he'd been doing all his life without knowing what to call it. Not with a word. With a look. "*You see it*", she'd said, and it had ruined him in a way that felt like the opposite of damage.

He crossed the apartment in three strides, flicked on the small lamp at his desk, and stood in the warm yellow bowl of it letting the storm's cold stay on his skin. The desk was a chaos of napkins and loose sheets and cheap sketchbooks with their spines broken. He'd stopped buying expensive paper when he realized ink chose the nearest surface no matter what he planned. He flattened a blank page with his palm and set the pen down gently.

Adrian started with her hair, because it had been the first thing to catch him. Not brown, not red, not the burnished copper he would normally reach for, but something that earned the word flaming without ever burning. He drew it loose, because that was how it had moved, as if it had remembered wind even inside the coffee shop.

Her dress came next. White and flowing, it was the simplest shape in the world but caressed her body like a hug. There was no seam he could see, no fastenings, no gaudy trim. It was elegant, just like her. The dress had moved like breath, like a thought. In the middle of his drawing he hesitated, but the pen somehow found the right lines for the way the fabric fell and the suggestion of the body beneath.

Eira was tall and statuesque with curves like those statues of Greek goddesses. Maybe that's what she was, a goddess. There was strength in the thickness of her thighs and the set of her shoulders, softness in the dip of her waist, and a feminine delicateness in her collarbone. He let himself be precise and then pulled back, because any attempt to pin her exactly to the page felt like an insult.

Her skin was easy in one sense and impossible in another. He had drawn every shade of human before, and he knew the difference between tan and gold was mostly the light. But there had been gold in her even under the café lamps, and the storm outside had made her glow like someone standing in a shrine. He shadowed the planes of her face with touches he knew he'd erase, because the truth of it was not the shape but the way seeing her made him feel something else.

Something that felt like longing. The goddess-like thing that flowed from her- he had no better phrase for it- wasn't power like electricity, but a divine essence that made him want to drop to his knees and bow before her. He saved her eyes for last because he didn't quite know how to draw those captivating eyes, and partly because he was afraid he would bring her to life once he did. A part of him felt as though creating her likeness on paper could summon her to his apartment. He knew it was a cowardly thought, but it was a thought he had, nonetheless.

He sketched the lids, the lashes, the tilt, and set the point of the pen against the paper where the iris would be. He thought green and the line stuttered. He thought gold and it felt false. Her eyes were a color he couldn't place, and it frustrated him to no end. He lifted the pen and let the point hover, waiting for his hand to do the thing it always did when he stopped thinking. Nothing came. He laughed once, quietly and without humor.

"All right," he said to the empty room. He set the pen down, rubbed his thumb and forefinger together to chase away the ache, and turned to the window. The storm was closer. Lightning broke and broke again, too regular to be chance, like a metronome set to a tempo he hated. The rain had thickened, and the street looked like a river with headlights.

Somewhere below, a siren shouted and then shut off. He pressed the ball of his hand against the glass and let the cold bleed up into his wrist.

"You're just a woman," he told himself, and felt stupid in the saying.

She had failed at hiding, and he had failed at not seeing. When she'd pulled him out of the car's path, when her fingers had closed on his arm, something ancient had hummed through his bones. He had felt impossibility pass through him like a chord. He could still recall where her grip had been if he closed his eyes: four perfect ovals like a temporary bruise made of warmth instead of pressure. He turned his wrist and looked in spite of himself. Nothing marked his skin.

He went back to the desk and flipped through older pages to avoid looking at the one he'd just made. The threads were there the way they always were, some in neat curves, some in tangles, some in patterns he could almost read if he let his eyes go unfocused.

Tonight, they made him think of the television in the café- the red banner, the way crowds looked when they became a single thing without meaning to. He had drawn a split earlier without knowing why. Now he saw the same jagged seam run through pages a month old, a year old. He traced it with a fingertip, felt foolish, and then felt afraid. He turned the page.

When he was ten, he'd woken from a dream with blood on his palm and no wound. He remembered the way his mother's mouth had pinched when she cleaned it, the way she'd said nothing. He'd drawn until he fell asleep that day. What he drew then looked a little like what lay before him now: a braid interrupted, a knot forming where it should not, a line that couldn't decide whether to go on or end.

He had wondered then if the world could come apart in a way a person could hear. Tonight, the storm answered yes. He put the old pages aside and forced himself to look at the new one: hair, dress, body, light, and those empty eyes, waiting.

He held the pen above them again, forever a fraction of an inch away. "You can't be angry with me," he said, and realized he wasn't talking to the paper.

"*What are you?*" he'd asked her in the rain, and she had not answered. He didn't expect her to say "goddess" and laugh it off. Instead, she'd turned her face half away and told him to stay alive, and it had felt more like a vow than a dismissal. He hated her for that. He loved her for it. He couldn't do either properly, and that felt like a thread too.

WHEN SLEEP FINALLY REACHED for him, he slid into its embrace. His head nodded over the desk, hand still on the page, his breath evening without his permission. He didn't move to the bed. He didn't turn off the lamp. The storm dimmed not at all, but his body surrendered despite it. He slipped into the narrow space dreams leave for waking people and found himself standing on a floor that wasn't floor at all.

It looked like water and held like glass. Lines ran beneath it in slow currents. When he stepped, something far below shivered. He was in a hall without walls; the ceiling was a sky that forgot to choose day or night. At the far end, three figures stood in a row, thin as reeds and taller than the space allowed. He could not tell if they faced him. He could not tell if they breathed. He told himself he didn't know them. He told himself three is a number like any other.

A loom rose out of nothing between them with no frame he could name, no material he could place, only the suggestion of tension and the whisper of fiber. Threads moved of their own accord. He saw one bright one he knew in a way that made his chest hurt, and before he could stop himself, he reached for it.

It burned without heat when his fingers brushed it and left nothing on his skin. He thought he heard a voice- just syllables, not a word- and the bright thread bowed toward him as if greeting. Another thread ran near it, darker and dense as a storm. When the bright one bowed, the other pulled taut. He felt their nearness like wind. He stepped closer and the floor rippled.

"*Don't,*" a woman's voice warned, and he couldn't tell which figure had spoken or if any had. The word came from everywhere like a tide going out. He froze, not out of obedience but because the sound had moved through his bones and left him hollow. A woman stood then where there had been no one, and of course it was her. Eira glided on the surface, the world beneath seeming crafted solely to carry her.

Her dress was white. Her hair flamed and refused to catch. Her skin held summer under a sky that had not decided what it was, and her eyes- well, he couldn't name them here either. They made him think of leaves and coins and the last light before dusk gives up. She stopped with an arm's length between them and looked at his outstretched hand. For a second, he thought she might take it.

Adrian longed to touch her face. To run a thumb across her bottom lip and place it to his lips. He wanted to be near her. Here, there, anywhere, it didn't matter. Some part of him desperately longed to be with her. He welcomed the feeling, because it felt natural, as if he were made *for* her.

The three tall figures shifted behind her, or perhaps the threads did. The bright line and the dark line vibrated like a plucked string. He felt the old ache in his head that meant he had drawn too long.

"*It isn't yours to touch,*" Eira said, and the words were gentler than any warning had a right to be.

"*I can see it,*" Adrian whispered, which felt like an excuse and a confession.

"*That doesn't make it safe,*" was her reply, and a thread shimmered as if agreeing.

He wanted to tell her he wasn't brave. He wanted to tell her he had been waiting his whole life to be told he was not insane. He wanted to tell her everything he'd never told anyone because it sounded ridiculous even in the mouth that owned it. Instead, he said, "*Are you real?*"

Something in her face softened at that, the tiniest easing around her mouth and the briefest flutter of her lashes. "*Yes,*" she said, and it sounded like the truth and a sentence both.

Behind her, one of the three figures raised a hand. The bright thread jerked as if something had nicked it. The dark thread snapped toward it and away, a motion that made him want to put his palm over his heart and hold it there. The floor under his feet sagged like he stood on the back of a sleeping animal that had just twitched.

"*Don't,*" came the voice again, its tone weighted with deeper menace. Eira turned her head that way in a gesture very like respect. When she looked back, he thought for a second that her eyes had chosen a color and then realized it was the light.

"*Wake,*" she said softly. And he did.

CHAPTER 5

ADRIAN

The lamp was still on. His neck hurt from the angle he'd slept in, and his mouth tasted like metal. He blinked, once, twice, and let the room come back around him in the ordinary ways: the smell of old coffee, the sound of pipes in the wall, the wind thinning to a steady hum as the storm moved off. He stared at the page beneath his hand, bracing for the usual humiliation of finding he'd drooled on it. He had not.

The lines he'd drawn before sleep had settled into themselves. Hair, dress, body and light, the eyes still unfinished. Below them, where the page had been blank, a single stroke had appeared, thin and true and decisive. Two curves meeting in a way he recognized without knowing why, the suggestion of a knot without the ugliness of tangle.

He lifted his hand and turned it over. A faint line, red as if newly irritated, ran across his palm where he'd touched the bright thread in the dream. He had the very brief, very useful thought that he should be frightened. He let it pass through him and sat very still until his breath stopped trying to flee.

"Okay," he said. He smiled then. Not wide, but real. It had been so long since his face eased into that simple expression that he almost chuckled aloud. It felt wrong on his face and good in his chest. "Okay."

He stood, stretched his back until something popped, and set a tea kettle on the stove. The blue flame watered the room with a different kind of light. He found a clean mug by choosing the least dirty option and swirled it with tap water to make himself feel better about it. While he waited for the boil, he did the thing he had decided nights ago he would stop doing. He made a plan.

It was not elaborate. It did not require him to be a version of himself he'd never met. He decided that he would go back to the coffee shop. He would go at the same hour. He would sit at the table near the door where she would have to see him if she came. He would bring paper he cared about and a pen that worked and the courage to shut up if she asked him to.

If she didn't come, he would leave after one cup and a reasonable amount of pretending. If she did, he would try to be the kind of person who deserved to be looked at the way she had looked at him, as if he were not a mistake.

The kettle clicked off. He poured, watched the steam pool and lift, and remembered the car and the sound tires make when they fail. He set the mug down and wrapped the fingers of one hand around the wrist she'd held.

"*It's dangerous for you to know me,*" she had said wearily. He could still hear her voice as she said it, soft and severe, the way a teacher who likes you might be when you're about to set your own work on fire. He had been stupid in the rain, saying things he would be ashamed to remember in the morning. "*It doesn't feel like I can forget you,*" he'd told her, because the truth had punched out of him like breath knocked out of a body. He flushed now, alone, thinking of it. He felt twelve. He felt ancient.

Adrian took the mug to the window and watched the edge of the storm pull itself away from the buildings. The sky cleared in a slow bruised bloom.

Somewhere below, in a city that didn't know his name, streetlights clicked from orange to white to nothing. He told himself he did not believe in omens. A moth hit the glass hard, a tiny thud like a fingertip rapping, and then clung there, shivering. He leaned in, amused despite himself, and saw that it wasn't a moth at all- just a leaf, wet and stuck, torn from a tree he couldn't identify by the way its veins made a map of it. He pressed the pad of his thumb to the other side of the glass, exactly where the leaf would be if the pane weren't there, and felt relief so sudden it made him laugh.

"You idiot," he said, and didn't mind that he meant himself.

ADRIAN WASHED the last of the ink off his hands, changed his shirt, and cut his hair with the patience of a person who had once drawn self-portraits to learn where lines belonged. He put on a jacket that fit and picked up his sketchbook, then stood in the doorway with the knob in his hand until the quiet of not moving sounded like a dare.

When he opened the door, a different wind met him. The city smelled scoured. The stairwell held the echo of rain long after it had stopped. He went down, hands in his pockets to keep from reaching for anything that wasn't there, and stepped into the morning that wasn't a morning yet. Neon signs flickered like eyelids, choosing to be awake. Above the rooftops, the clouds trailed away in long strips like torn cloth.

He walked toward Seventh and Willow without telling himself that was what he was doing. He passed a bakery where someone had started the ovens an hour too early and another where they never turned them off. Sugar drifted on the air, and with it came an unexpected lightness in his mood. A woman he didn't know nodded at him as if she did. A man with a dog let the leash go slack and the dog chose not to run. The world, in that precise ten-minute window before the day admits it is day, acted like it would continue.

At the corner, the coffee shop's lights glowed against the glass like a soft commandment. He stood on the opposite curb for a beat longer than necessary and then crossed as if obeying. Inside, the red-haired barista with the lightning-bolt tattoo was propping the door with a rubber wedge. She smiled vaguely the way morning people do when they're choosing to be kind.

"You're early," she said, and her face lit up as usual as she took him in. She was a beautiful woman, he could admit that, but he felt nothing for anyone but the mysterious woman he'd met the other day. *Eira.*

"Couldn't sleep," he said, and she made the you-and-me-both face and turned away. He went to the table near the door because that was the plan. He set the sketchbook down, the good paper on top, and put the napkins in a neat stack to punish them for being what they were.

He did not look at the booth where she had been. He looked at his hands, which behaved. He drew a line down the page to surrender to the need to make a mark, and then drew another, and found that they wanted to curve. He let them. The pattern that came was softer than last night's, less jagged, as if the city had agreed to a truce with itself for an hour. He watched the first crossing grow and thought of the dream again-the three figures, the loom that wasn't, the bright and the dark threads bowing and pulling.

The door sighed, and Adrian looked up without deciding to. For a second, disappointment made his chest go shallow. It was only light, shifting because someone walked past outside, and a jogger's reflection was like a smear. He laughed at himself under his breath and returned to the paper.

When she came, he didn't notice her by sight. He *felt* her presence, which sounded like a ridiculous thing to say even in the confines of his own head. But something in the room shifted. The chatter softened, the refrigerator's hum grew still, and a coolness slipped into the space between his face and the page. He lifted his eyes and there she was, and he forgave himself instantly for every stupid thing he'd ever thought.

She stood just inside the door, radiating the goddess-like energy he had noticed when they last met. He waged a silent war within himself, resisting the force that drew him toward her. She wore a delicate white dress, not the same as last time. Her hair burned against the dim light, and her luminous skin reduced the gold pendant on the woman nearby to the shade of brass. Her eyes chose a color only while they held him, abandoning it the instant they looked away.

Eira's mere presence, her essence, was undeniable. Goddess wasn't a word he could say without flinching. He said it anyway, to himself, and waited to see if the ceiling fell. It didn't. The barista said "good morning" to a new patron and meant it. A man by the window laughed at something on his phone. The world held.

Eira met his gaze and did not look away. The corner of her mouth lifted in acknowledgment, not invitation. He felt the place where her fingers had closed on his arm remember their shape. He stood before he knew he had, which would have embarrassed him if it had happened for anyone else.

"Hi," he said, lifting his hand in a half-wave, a sudden lump catching in his throat. This woman stirred something in him to the point where he found it hard to speak.

"Good morning, Adrian" Eira said, and there was warmth in her voice this time.

He wanted to say, *I dreamed you.* He wanted to say, *I'm not crazy.* He wanted to say, *I don't know the rules, but I'll learn them if you tell me they exist.* Instead, he said, "I saved you a seat," and hated and loved himself at the same time for the way the sentence landed between them.

Eira glanced at the empty chair across from him, then back at him. For a heartbeat, the air tightened the way it does when a storm decides whether to strike again. Then she moved toward him, and the room exhaled. When she sat, he thought the table might be smaller than it had been a second ago. He pushed the sketchbook aside to make space for a cup she did not have yet, and felt her look drop to the page. He braced to be ashamed.

"You tried again," she said. "I told you to stay away and you decided to come closer."

She wore the most beautiful frown, he thought, her mouth turning downward as her eyes roamed over his face. He let out a breath he hadn't realized he was holding.

"I couldn't resist," he said, the truth slipping through his lips like water from a cracked glass. "I haven't stopped thinking about you since we met. I don't even understand why..." His voice trailed off as he looked away, heat rising in his cheeks.

Her eyes settled on the sketch's unfinished gaze. He expected her to mock it, but she only nodded, as if that was exactly how she should be drawn.

"You shouldn't," she said, almost apologetically. "But I understand, and I don't fault you for it. The universe has a way of making itself known."

"Shouldn't because it's bad," he said, frowning "or shouldn't because...you don't *want* me to?" He waved a hand at the world. She didn't answer that.

"You came early," she said instead, like a person choosing kindness when truth is too heavy to move.

"So did you," he said. Something like amusement flickered across her face and he wanted to trap it in amber and keep it on a shelf.

"I don't usually come here often," she said, "And I can't say that I'm a morning person."

"Me either." he replied, enjoying how easily conversation flowed between them. "I came because I haven't been sleeping well lately. I needed a distraction."

For a moment they only looked at each other, breathing in the weight of the silence.

"Do you drink coffee?" he blurted, and instantly wanted to sink into the floor. "I mean, obviously, it's a coffee shop, but-"

"I do," she said with a soft smile, rescuing him, if that was what that was. "Today, perhaps."

He rose a little too quickly, eagerness carrying him forward, and went to the counter to order two of the drinks he always chose because he wanted to impress her, even if only with the gesture. The barista looked at him with the fondness people reserve for regulars who try.

When he brought the cups back, the steam made his eyes water. He set one near her hand and said nothing about the way it shook.

"Thank you," she said, wrapping her fingers around the mug with the same careful delicacy he had imagined she possessed. He should have let the quiet be what it was. He should have drunk and waited. He should have kept his hands still on the table and not reached for anything that didn't belong to him. Instead, he put his palm on the paper and heard his mouth say, as if he'd rehearsed it, "Don't tell me not to remember you. It won't work."

Color moved in her eyes like a decision. "It isn't about memory," she said. "It's about cost."

He swallowed. "Yours or mine?" She looked at the sketch again. "Both. Everything has a price."

Outside, the last of the storm dragged its dark belly along the edge of the sky and moved on. Inside, somebody laughed, and the sound landed like a bell. Adrian looked at Eira and thought of the strange knot on the page that had drawn itself while he slept. He did not know anything that mattered beyond staring into the eyes of this woman, the woman whose eye color he did not yet have a name for.

It was as if his mind fumbled for the word, almost knew, but slipped away like running water in a stream.

"Okay," he said, forcing his voice to be steady. "Tell me what not to do."

She looked at him for a long, careful beat, and then she did the most natural thing he had seen her do- she laughed, small and startled and almost shy, as if he'd handed her something easier than she expected to hold. Then she cleared her throat and transformed her face into a serious expression.

"Don't follow me when I leave," she said.

He nodded. "I can do that."

"Don't touch what you see when you dream." She said, firmly.

Adrian's mouth went dry. "Wait-how do you know... Can you-?"

"Yes," she interrupted, and there was no above or below in it, only exactly as much as needed. "I know."

He breathed once, and then again. "Okay. I won't ask, but that's a bit... strange. I'm sorry, you go on."

He was starting to get flustered, which is something that never happened to him when he spoke to women. But she wasn't an ordinary woman, not by any means.

"And don't," she added, softer, "try to draw my eyes."

He looked at the page and laughed without meaning to. "Too late."

"Then stop," she said, reaching out and gently touching his hand. He put the pen down. The touch felt like prayer. Like a spark of electricity danced between the place where her hand touched his and opened a pathway directly to his soul.

They drank coffee neither of them needed and let conversation carry the time as the day climbed the windows like a rising tide. When she stood, he stayed seated. When she touched the back of the chair with her fingertips, his skin remembered the shape of his own arm beneath her hand. When she looked at him last, he had to fight the urge to go back on his word and follow her. He wasn't sure what was happening, but this woman was wrecking him in the best way.

Adrian watched her go and did not follow her. He watched the door close and did not count the seconds to see if the glass would shiver. He looked down at the page and saw that the eyes still waited, and that the knot he hadn't drawn had tightened a fraction more. He turned to a clean sheet and drew a line that wanted to be a curve. This time, he let it.

CHAPTER 6

EIRA

The veil between the mortal realm and that of the Sovereign thinned like gossamer between her fingers as Eira drifted along its edges. She had not meant to come here. Her domain still trembled, and her siblings' warnings lingered like echoes in her chest. Fury's scorn. Melora's pity, and her solemn words, *"If you love him, he will be the one to pay."*

She had sworn she would stay away. Sworn she would not falter again. And yet she found herself moving, weightless between realms, searching not with her eyes but with her essence. Searching for him. Adrian.

His apartment met her with the soft insistence of warm light and old paint. The air held the sharp- sweet edge of turpentine and the damp scent of rain sneaking in through a cracked window. Canvases leaned shoulder to shoulder along the wall, a narrow trail of bare floor threaded between jars of brushes, tubes of color, and the soft drift of paper napkins he never stopped using. A lamp with a dented shade turned one corner honey-gold and left the rest to the blue hush of the city outside.

Adrian was there, as she knew he would be, with his back turned, sleeves shoved to his elbows, a streak of sap green dried along the tendon of his wrist. The brush in his hand moved and stopped, moved and stopped, like a heartbeat trying to choose its pace. He stared at the canvas as if it were speaking. He was painting her, and it was the most beautiful painting she had ever seen.

The fact that he had memorized every detail about her to make this painting almost took her breath away. She knew she should leave. She knew she should do anything but stay and watch. The brush lifted, his shoulders changed, and she saw the moment he felt her.

He didn't turn at first, keeping his face toward the canvas as art flowed through his skillful fingers. Then he set the brush against the tray and spoke her name, quiet and certain, as if he were finishing a line he'd started hours ago.

"Eira." He whispered it almost like a prayer, one she wished she could answer.

She stepped far enough into the lamplight to be real, her voice echoing his greeting. "Adrian."

He turned and those dark, fathomless eyes found her, and for a breath she felt the pull of them like a tide. He didn't reach for her the way he wanted to, only looked, and that steadied something in her that had been shaking all day.

"You came," he said. No triumph, no accusation. A simple fact reframed as gratitude.

"I was near," she said, and a lump formed in her throat at the half-truth. "This seemed a good moment."

He glanced at the canvas. "It's my best time," he admitted. "When the city's quiet and the light's wrong for anything else." He smiled with one corner of his mouth. "And when I'm alone."

"Are you?" she asked, knowing the answer and needing to hear it anyway.

"Mostly," he said. "But that feels less true when you're here."

She ought to have gone. Sorrow had warned her gently, but Fury had not. Eira could feel the edge of consequence even now. There was something in the room noticing, pausing, waiting to be sure. She dimmed herself further. The lamp wavered once and held.

"May I?" she asked, gesturing toward a clear patch of floor near the easel.

He blinked. "You want to sit?" He glanced at the only chair and then at the mess. "I can clean this up-give me a second-" he stumbled over his words as he scrambled around, attempting to clean the space.

"It's all right," she said, smiling with a grace that made him feel out of place in proximity to her. "This is a nice place." She looked around, her eyes drinking in every detail of his small apartment.

Adrian hesitated for a moment then cleared a seating area, his eyes settling on the paint-stained rug that he wished he had attempted to clean. Outside, tires hissed on wet pavement. Somewhere above, a neighbor laughed.

He gestured toward the apartment. "You're so patient with me, even when I'm all over the place. I want to ask how you got here, but I think we're past those kinds of questions. Not that you'd answer." He let out a soft chuckle at his own words.

"You are patient with me," she said. "I come and go. It's my nature, and there are things that I just can't change. And you're right, I won't answer that." Then she smiled, brighter than he had ever known her to smile.

"I can handle that," he said, then added, "Do you want tea? I don't have sugar. Just honey."

"Yes, I'd like that," she said in a lighter tone than he'd heard from her. "Tea happens to be one of my favorites."

He rose and crossed the small kitchen in four strides, turning his back to the comfort of his hands knowing what to do. Water, kettle, the small music of a spoon finding a mug. She watched him move and found herself ensnared as her eyes roamed his shoulders, broad under a soft shirt, the line of his spine, the easy power in him that had nothing to do with what he looked like and everything to do with how he inhabited space, as if rooms remembered him.

He came back carrying two mugs, placing one carefully at her side. Their fingers did not touch, but Eira wished they did. Honey gathered in a gold oval at the bottom as steam fogged the air between them. She wrapped her hands around the heat and brought the mug to her lips, sipping the delicious liquid.

"I told you not to paint my eyes," she reminded him softly.

"I didn't," he said with a shake of his head, tilting it toward the unfinished canvas. "See? I'm following orders. Not exactly my style. What are you doing to me?" He said it like a joke, but the weight behind it was real.

"It suits you," she said with a sly smile. "Men who listen are so hard to find." He smiled as he watched her, admiring her beauty. Then he broke the silence.

"Will you tell me something? A true thing. Not... everything. Just something only you can tell me."

Eira could have lied. The veil was designed to make lies sound gentle. She could have borrowed a story from some mortal woman and given Adrian nothing true of herself. Instead she watched the steam lift from the mug and answered as if she were telling him a secret she meant to keep.

Her lips curved. "One true thing? I hate the sound of clocks. Even when they're soft, I feel like they're chasing me. I wish I could destroy every clock everywhere."

He blinked, a quiet laugh escaping him. "Strange, but real. Don't get me started on alarm clocks."

"Strange is safer than the truths I can't give," she murmured, tracing the rim of her mug with one finger.

"I don't know," he said, leaning forward. "Feels honest to me. Like you just told me what keeps you awake at night."

Her eyes flicked up to meet his. "And what keeps you awake?"

He hesitated, then shrugged with a crooked smile. "Faces I can't forget. Conversations I never finished. You."

Silence hung between them for a breath too long, and she looked away, but the corner of her mouth betrayed her with the faintest smile. He had spoken aloud what she had sensed from him all along.

"Careful," she said. "That sounded almost like two true things."

He chuckled, low and nervous. "Then maybe I owe you a secret, just to balance it out."

Silence stretched between them for a beat, then Adrian spoke. "What are you called?"

"I am called by my name, Eira," she said, letting him hear the oldest ring in it. Snow, peace, dawn, a word carried through a dozen languages that had touched her and stayed. "But I know what you actually mean to ask. Where I am from, I am called the Sovereign. One of many."

He nodded as if that answered more than a question.

"It fits," he said, and looked at the canvas. "And I want to know more. I want to know everything about you, but I'm not going to ask too many questions that I know you won't answer."

"Well," she said. "It seems like you're finally listening."

He almost laughed, caught himself, and smiled. "You have a habit of speaking in riddles. I'm trying to keep up." He set the mug down, careful not to stain the carpet with honey. "Can I ask you something else?"

"You may ask." Eira said, relaxed in a way that made Adrian's chest tighten. They were growing too close, too comfortable for him not to crave her presence.

"Why are you here now?" he asked. "You could come any time. You said not to follow you. You told me not to draw your eyes and not to touch what I see when I dream. And I listened- mostly." He grimaced, glancing at the canvas. "So why tonight?"

She could feel Balance leaning, curious but not yet cruel. Speak carefully, the calm in her said. Speak true as far as you can, and then stop.

"Because the city is quiet," she said. "Because quiet is a door, and you were standing in it. Because you paint me as if I am real, even when I am...less so."

"Less so?" His brow pulled together. "You're the most...something person I've ever met. I've never met anyone like you... and I'm starting to realize that's a good thing."

She let that warm her in a place the storm hadn't reached. "I shouldn't stay long," she said softly.

"I know," he said, and his voice stayed even. He was learning. "Then let's not spend it asking you questions you can't answer."

"What would you like to do instead?" she asked.

"Talk like strangers who are pretending to be friends," he said, grinning now, "or friends pretending to be strangers." He tilted his head. "Tell me about the first place that felt like yours."

She let her gaze go unfocused for a moment and chose something that would not break anything to say aloud.

"A courtyard," she said after a pause. "The stones were always warm from the sun. There were pomegranate trees, and I remember how they would split open on the branches. A fountain ran all day, and I used to listen to it like it was breathing. There was a woman who sat with me sometimes. She taught me things about cooking, about her children. I was younger then. Smaller."

Adrian sat very still, listening attentively. "That's sounds like a fond memory."

They both smiled at that.

"It is," she said, and sipped the tea. "I haven't made new memories in a very, very long time." Eira smiled sadly, meeting his gaze.

There was a long pause before she asked him to reciprocate.

"Mine was the back stairwell of an apartment building," he said. "Cinderblock painted the wrong shade of beige. It was cool in summer and warm in winter, and the lights buzzed in a way that sounded like the city was thinking. I'd sit on the third step because no one used it and draw on my knees. I liked that I could hear people on the other stairwell, and they couldn't hear me." He smiled without lifting his mouth. "I guess that sounds sad."

"Not really," she said, thoughtfully. "It sounds like something that gives you comfort."

He nodded once, grateful. "What about music?" he asked, lighter. "Do you have a favorite?"

"I like lullabies," she said gently, tilting her head as she smiled fondly, "The old kind. You wouldn't have ever heard of them. They always had strange promises, like the sea wouldn't take you if you slept. My favorite one was about stones being gentle if you asked them to."

He laughed cheerfully, the sound reverberating throughout her body. "So you're telling me you used to negotiate with rocks?" His smile was so genuine, so inviting that she couldn't help but return it.

"Only when no one's listening," she whispered conspiratorially, a sly grin spreading across her face.

"Then you do," he said, satisfied. "I whistle when I can't sit still, and I hum when I don't want to cry. There are so many things in my head sometimes that just overlap. It's really infuriating at times."

She gave him the smallest nod, and he went on. "Okay, your turn. Tell me a word you like to say."

She considered it. "Mercy," she said at last. "In any language, it takes courage to ask for it."

He let the silence go on for a beat before responding. "That's heavier than I expected. I was thinking... I don't know...coffee?" He laughed merrily, running his strong hands through his hair.

"Actually, let me try that again. If I had to really think..." he tapped his fingers gently against his lip, letting silence stretch for a beat. "I'd go with 'keep,'" he said, running a distracting thumb over his bottom lip. "It's greedy and tender at the same time. Like when you're asking someone to stay with you because you want to keep them. So, yeah, keep." He tilted his head thoughtfully, as his eyes bore into hers. Adrian could feel the tension building between them, and the budding of something neither of them would name yet.

The lamp hummed, and somewhere a pipe clicked in the wall as the city took a breath. Adrian shifted, set his empty mug aside, and reached for the rag on the floor, wiping the green from his wrist with a gentleness that made the gesture look like care rather than cleaning.

"I had an art teacher," he began, "She didn't touch my drawings. She put her hand near them and then used her other hand to hold her wrist back." He smiled, remembering the exact angle of it. "She said, 'I don't want to put my fingerprints on your ghosts.' I thought that was stupid then. I think about it once a week now."

"What did you draw for her?" Eira asked, curiously.

"The same things," he said, thoughtfully. "Threads. I called them maps of places I'd never been to yet. She called them structures. My mother called them worrying." He scrubbed at the paint that didn't want to leave his skin. "Someone at a gallery once said they bothered her. She meant it as a kindness. It was. Sometimes I think I'm too attuned to the wrong kinds of attention to be properly angry."

"You endure," Eira continued, focusing on those midnight eyes, "Because endurance is something you were given and not a thing you choose." He looked at her, surprised by the shape of that truth.

"Wow." Adrian inhaled, his eyes settling on hers as he spoke, "You make it easy to say true things."

"It is my nature." She said, catching herself a breath before she said something she shouldn't. "Adrian, I think you succeed more than you fail." She said this with more confidence in him than he felt.

"I don't know how to measure that," he said, dropping his head.

"You wouldn't," she said softly. "It isn't given to you to know. But I've seen enough of you to know that you will be successful in anything you do. There is fire within you. Don't ever let anyone extinguish that."

He looked at her for a long time. "Sometimes I think you're very young," he paused before continuing, "and then you say something like that."

They both laughed at that, wrapped up in that short moment of happiness. She genuinely found that she enjoyed his company, and she knew, deep down, that this would cost her. She felt the tug toward confession like tide against ankle bones. *Tell him what you are! Tell him why you can't... tell him the Law was written to keep the world from turning inside out.*

The lamp flickered, silence creeping between them again before she spoke. "I am both," she said, but her tone was guarded and barely above a whisper. "A great deal of old and a great deal of new, all at once."

"That," he said, "is the strangest thing you've said tonight. I like it."

He picked up the brush again and held it like a thought. "If I ask you too much, will it cause you any harm?"

"It might," she said honestly. "But not tonight."

"Would you tell me if it did?" His voice gentled on the edge of the question.

"I will tell you when it does," she said, nodding her head.

Adrian nodded, and the gratitude in that small motion made her chest ache. He turned the canvas a fraction and touched the brush to a place far from the eyes, at the hem of the dress where it pooled like fog. He added a shadow that wasn't darker so much as deeper. He lightened the air just to the left of her shoulder. He watched her in the glass of the window rather than directly, and Eira felt the rightness of that, like the way mortals sometimes know to look slantwise at holy things.

"What color would you name your eyes," he asked, still not looking at them, "if you had to choose?"

"I don't," she said. "But if I did, it wouldn't be in a language you could pronounce."

He laughed, low. "Fair."

"What would you name yours?" she asked. "Night water," he said without thinking, and then made a face. "That's ridiculous."

"It is," she agreed, pleased. "And correct. They remind me of pools of midnight."

He touched the brush to the canvas again, soft as a breath. "If I asked you for one more true thing," he said, "would you give it?"

"If I can," she said, finding that she didn't mind sharing more of herself with this man. This mortal, whose presence could calm any chaos stirring inside her.

"What should I be afraid of?" he asked. He did not look at her this time. Instead, he watched the place where paint met canvas.

She pondered this a moment, before sighing softly. "Nothing if you stay away from me. Everything if you don't."

Eira could have said Balance. She could have said gods. She thought of his dream and the bright and dark threads bowing. She remembered Sorrow's warning, the words ringing like a bell. *If you love him, he will be the one to pay.* Eira didn't know what she would decide, but she knew that she felt a pull towards Adrian that was hard to ignore. Impossible, almost.

The city outside shifted from blue to something nearer to gray. The radiator ticked, and Eira knew that she had overstayed her welcome in this realm with this man.

"I should go," she said, rising gracefully. She didn't want to, but she knew she had overstayed her visit.

"I know," he said. He set the brush down and stood. He didn't offer a hand, because he was learning the shape of her presence, but his body wanted to reach out. She stepped back far enough that the room could exhale.

"I won't follow you," he said, solemn as a vow.

"Thank you, Adrian" she said, and his name on her lips sounded like life.

He glanced at the canvas, at those unfinished eyes. "I'll leave them," he said.

"Good," she replied kindly. "Some doors should stay closed until they are not."

He huffed a laugh. "That's the kind of sentence that will keep me up at three in the morning."

She moved toward the place where the air thinned. The veil loosened under her palm like silk waking. She looked back and found him looking at her with that careful awe that never felt like worship, only witness.

"Be safe, wherever you go. But please Eira- come back to me." he said, realizing that he didn't know when he would see her again. He felt a twinge of sorrow at that thought. "I just- I'd like-..." the word died on his lips as he nodded his head instead, running his hands through his hair. He didn't need to finish that sentence, because Eira understood what he meant. Stay safe. Stay whole. Stay in the world in a way that does not break you for me.

"I will try," she said. "I'd like to see you again as well."

When Eira stepped through, the apartment held its shape behind her. The lamp continued its humming, and paint continued drying. The Balance did not lash but watched as it always did, and waited.

On the floor, the napkin he had turned over to tell her a story had slid, unnoticed, against her foot and gone with her. In her realm, it fell like a leaf onto still water and floated there, a mortal scrap in a place that had never held paper before. The willows bent toward it, curious. Eira watched the ink begin to blur and did not lift it out.

Back in his apartment, Adrian stood very still until the tightness in his chest loosened. He made another cup of tea, turned the canvas an inch, and did not touch the eyes. He drew a single line in the air with his finger where no paint would ever go, naming nothing, claiming nothing, and let it dissolve like breath. He could think of nothing but the sound of Eira's voice, her beautiful face, and the way her words sounded strange, as if from another time period.

The city surrendered its quiet by inches. He listened as it did, the way a person listens for a familiar footstep in a hall, and smiled when he caught himself doing it. He had not been promised anything. He had been given the smallest piece of truth and the tenderness to hold it. He decided, carefully, to be kind to the space she'd left behind. He opened a window. He washed the mug. He put the green-stained rag in the sink to soak. When he sat again, he drew the simplest of shadows beneath the hem of her dress so she would not be standing on nothing, even in paint.

"Be safe," he said once more, to no one in particular and exactly the right person because he had a feeling the words would carry themselves to her.

CHAPTER 7
EIRA

Eira had always been careful when crossing the veil. She was careful to keep her steps light, her essence dimmed, and her stillness cloaked. But lately, caution had worn thin. She no longer lingered at the border, testing for resistance, but passed more freely than she should.

What began as rare visits became a habit. She made more trips to the mortal world than she ever had before. A tether pulled her back to the mortal world again and again, and each time it grew harder to sever. The mortal realm was a loud, flawed, breathing thing and she found herself hungering for it.

She looked around, taking in the sight of her own realm betraying her. The water in her domain, once still as glass, now rippled of its own accord. The horizon quivered faintly as though dawn had grown unsteady. The willows bent too low, branches brushing the mirrored surface like hands too heavy with dew. Peace had never trembled before. Now it did. But Eira was not there to watch it falter. She was here, among the mortals.

The city lived beneath her feet. She walked its streets cloaked in her veil, simple and inconspicuous, her white dress blending into shadows that should have hidden her but never quite did. She let her senses drink in the hiss of a bus braking at the corner; the warm bite of roasted chestnuts from a vendor's cart, the sudden laughter of a group of students spilling out of a bar. It was disorder, color, and noise. And yet it was alive.

In her realm, Peace was stillness. Here, peace was fragile, flickering, argued over, fought for. Here, peace breathed. And then there was Adrian. She could feel that she *was* peace for him.

He painted late, always late, as if night itself belonged to him. His apartment glowed like a hearth in the dark, lamplight spilling over canvases stacked against walls. Eira slipped in quietly, never knocking. She stood at the edge of the room and watched him. His hair was tied up in a knot atop his head giving her a complete view of his beautiful face. A tendril of loose hair brushed his jaw as he leaned forward, deep in concentration.

The brush moved steady in his hand, his wrist flexing with strength and precision. His shirt was unbuttoned at the throat, sleeves rolled past his elbows, the faint sheen of sweat on his golden skin from the closeness of the lamp. He painted her again. He always did. By now he had close to a dozen sketches and paintings of her, always from different angles, pulled from memory.

The auburn hair he'd captured on canvas came to life through paint. Her shoulders curved delicately, her figure tall, commanding and yet tender. Always, he left the eyes unfinished. He paused often, as though sensing her even when veiled. Sometimes he would turn, look toward the shadows where she stood. And though she said nothing, his lips curved faintly, because somehow he knew she was there.

This was why she stayed. The simple act of being near him, watching his hands while he worked, hearing the scratch of bristles on canvas, listening to the kettle whistle softly in the kitchen, all seemed to steady her. And yet, each time, it fractured her further.

· · ·

ADRIAN

Adrian knew she was there. He always knew. He dipped his brush, set color to canvas, but his attention stretched beyond the lines. The hair on his arms lifted, that same pressure in the air when a storm is waiting. He didn't look directly because if he did, he feared she would vanish like smoke in the wind. Instead, he worked, and let the knowledge of her burn quietly inside him. She was impossible. Otherworldly. He couldn't explain it, not even to himself.

He had tried, in the weeks since the rainstorm, through sketches scrawled in margins, notes scribbled in the dark but none of them sufficed. He had written her name in fancy script on pages, and even those words on pages looked ancient and divine. He felt foolish for going to that extreme when he barely knew her. But when she breathed, when she moved, the air bent. And yet she sat sometimes with a mug between her hands, listening to his rambling stories about subway musicians and the smell of wet brick after a storm.

She would laugh so softly, like dawn breaking. Or she would tilt her head, listening so intently he felt every word mattered. Who was she, this woman who came and went like mist? He painted her not because he wanted to, but because his very soul had the impulse to do so. And every time the eyes eluded him. He feared that if he painted them, she would become real, and then he would lose her. He glanced at the canvas. The figure waited there, half-finished. Behind him, the air shifted faintly. He smiled, not turning.

"I know you're here," he whispered. "I always know when you're here."

As if in response, the lamp flickered once.

FURY

Across realms, storms raged too soon. Fury's domain was a forge of thunder with skies black with fire clouds, plains where lightning struck like hammers on anvils. Here, the air burned red, the ground cracked and smoking. Bolts tore into the earth unbidden. His warriors, those mortal souls who carried his fury in battle, woke restless, sharpening blades against stone with no enemy nearby.

Thamys stood at the cliff's edge, his cloak whipping like flame. He snarled. *This was not my doing.* He felt the rift stretch throughout his realm, leaving tears of destruction in its wake. Not in his domain alone, though. Somewhere, Peace was unanchored. And her breaking fed his rage.

MERCY

Elestra sat in her silver hall, a place of moonlight and quiet fountains. Her gown shimmered with pearls, her veil thin as water. Normally her hands soothed, silver light flowing to mend wounds of body and spirit. Tonight, they trembled. A man knelt before her, confessing sins she had not asked to hear. Her mercy had spilled too soon, loosening his tongue, drowning him in guilt. She pulled back, appalled at her own power turned cruel. Tears welled, slipping beneath her veil. She pressed her hands together.

"Peace," she whispered, sorrow trembling her voice. "What have you done?"

JOY

Lysera twirled in her garden, her dress gold, hair crowned with flowers. Normally laughter burst around her, dancers spinning, bells ringing bright. But now her flowers bloomed too quickly, wilting within hours. The bells gave hollow sounds. Her dancers stumbled, joy leaving them mid-step. She pressed a hand to her chest.

"Sister," she murmured. "Do not falter. You take me with you."

DEATH

Thaloré stood in the marble hall by the endless river, robes black, crown bone, his pale eyes watching souls drift past. The current, normally smooth, now faltered. Some souls came too quickly, cut short. Others clung to bodies longer than they should, stubborn, defiant. Death did not sigh. He did not rage. But his gaze lifted. He felt Peace wavering. And when Peace wavered, all things did. When the balance of one shifted, all of the Sovereign felt it. This was their nature by design. He sighed heavily, knowing what he must do next.

Eira

Back in the mortal world, Eira felt it. She had been spending so much time with Adrian that she had begun to ignore her duty, the task she was burdened with since the dawn of all things. The kettle in Adrian's kitchen screamed though no one had set it to boil. The light above them flickered and cracked, glass fracturing down its length. Outside, shouts rose, horns blared, and a fight erupted in the street below.

Adrian looked up from his canvas confused, eyes widening. "What do you think is going on out there?"

Eira's heart clenched. She knew this was coming, but she hadn't fully prepared herself for the weight of the consequences.

"The beginning of the end," she admitted softly, letting out a small sigh.

The Balance pressed against her, heavy, unseen. Threads tugged. Somewhere, the Loom shifted. She should leave. She should return to her waters, steady them before they broke apart. But she did not move. She stayed in the apartment with him, her hands placed gently in his, her pulse a song she could not silence.

Far above, the Loom shivered. Two threads, one bright and one dark, bent toward one another. The smallest knot began to form. The Weavers' hands hovered, their scissors gleaming. The Fates did not speak. They never did. But their silence was heavier than thunder.

CHAPTER 8
THE SOVEREIGNS

The Convergence chamber belonged to no single realm. It was built where the threads ran closest to the surface of the world, a circular hall of pale stone open to every horizon at once. Through its high arches a dozen skies looked in, a storm over iron seas, auroras combing polar dark, a summer noon that never moved, and beneath all that light the floor shone like black water veined with slow pulses of silver. At the center hovered the Loom: not timber, not iron, but a living net of filaments, each thread a color language had never separated, gliding and tightening with a patience older than time.

The Sovereign came the way seasons arrive, one after another, yet somehow all at once. Thamys, called Fury, strode in first in helmless armor scored by heat, a cloak like banked coals trailing from one shoulder. Sparks guttered from the nails of his boots when they struck the obsidian floor. He would not sit. He paced the curve, jaw set, eyes molten as he watched the Loom.

Melora, known as Sorrow, followed in silence, her indigo robes trailing behind her. Silver lined the partings of her dark hair. The bells sewn into her hem did not ring, for Sorrow moves too gently for noise. She took her seat with the grave ceremony of one arriving at a vigil never meant to end.

Elestra, known as Mercy, entered veiled in pale silk with pearls sewn like dew to the gauze across her hair. Her hands glowed faintly as if moonlight had caught in her bones. She clasped them to steady their tremor and bowed her head toward the Loom before sitting.

Lysera came diminished, her gold dress that once threw off sunlight now muted to soft straw. Thick curls that should have been riotous settled in tired spirals, and her anklet bells that usually sung for her gave only a tired shake. She smiled as she always did, and for the first time in eons, her smile looked like work.

Akria, who was Pain, wore red in clean, severe lines. Her hair was a brilliant black knot at the nape, her mouth a quiet blade. She had brought no ornament, only a narrow ring of onyx on one finger that turned as she thought. She did not look at anyone when she sat, instead choosing to study the floor as if it might confess.

Sedara drifted in velvet the color of wine seen through candle-light. The perfume at her throat was faint and wicked. She glanced once at Fury with amusement, then lounged as though the chair had learned to please her.

Vireth took his place without ceremony, draped in black leather close cut, a cloak like a shadow he'd sharpened himself. He threaded a gloved hand across the table's edge, tapping once, twice-counting or threatening, it was never clear.

Zivael, that which had always been known as Life, arrived in a gown the green of first leaves rinsed by rain, her hair crowned with small open blooms. Her presence softened the chamber, bringing a warmth that lingered despite the temperaments filling it.

Thaloré, Death, came last as he always did, not because he was late but because the room learned silence from him. His robe was black sewn with a map of small constellations, and a thin circlet of bone lay in his dark hair. His eyes were the pale gray of river mist. When he crossed the threshold, even Fury stopped pacing.

The doors opened once more. Eira entered with the hush of rivers. Her dress was white and unadorned, its hem a whisper. Her auburn hair fell in loose waves, and her eyes, a mix of every color yet almost-gold, held the color of the Loom reflected. She was Peace, and the chamber knew her. Yet her stillness was wrong around the edges, a held breath that didn't smooth. They did not rise for her. None rose for any. But they watched as she crossed to the empty chair at the circle's edge and did not sit.

Thaloré's voice carried throughout the room, the sound enough to silence the wind. "The Convergence is convened."

Fury leaned on his fists, cloak burning a slow red. His hostile energy was palpable, felt throughout the chamber. "We waste time waiting to name what all of us feel. Balance wails. My storms break their leashes. Her crossings made this." He pointed a pale accusing finger at Eira, causing her to inhale sharply.

Eira lifted her chin. "You mean my visits to the mortal realm."

"Your trespass," Vireth said, the word precise.

"Your yearning," Sedara purred, as if tasting a sweet.

"Your ache," Melora whispered, and that one reached Eira deep in her bones. She felt it land like a hand at the back where grief places its palm.

Zivael's voice was soft, warm as the first hour after rain. "And your witness," she added. "Peace has always walked among mortals. It is not new to her."

"It is new in this shape," Akria said. Her onyx ring began to glow a faint red, possibly drinking in Eira's inner turmoil. "The pulse of pain in the human cities has altered. Some wounds close too quickly, others fester. That is not her ordinary presence."

Lysera folded her hands around her knee. The bells on her ankle made a tired sound. "Laughter dies halfway across a room. Then, somewhere else, strangers share bread and no one knows why. It is not...balanced."

Elestra's veil lifted when she drew breath. "Forgiveness spills where it is not asked and dries where it is begged," she said, almost to herself. "I put my hands on a woman who had done great harm and watched her weep because my mercy came too soon. That is not how it ought to be."

Eira's fingers tightened at her sides, her patience turning to anger. Did they not know what this was costing *her*? "I know the ripples. I feel them first."

"Then confess," Fury snapped. "Acknowledge the law broken and we can pass our sentence."

Thaloré did not look away from Eira. "There will be no sentence before we hear the whole. We will not condemn our sister."

Revenge's fingers went still. "What 'whole' is there? She descended, uninvited! Revealed power, and jeopardized all of our realms- she spared a life due to end! The code is clear." He was quiet, but his anger was palpable, taking on a life of its own.

"The code is also clear that motive informs remedy," Zivael said, unruffled. "Not because we are soft, brother, but because we are exact. But I do agree, we should pass judgment before matters are taken to the Fates- or the Architect."

Stillness blanketed the room with that. No one in the chamber desired to meet with the Fates, good occasion or bad.

"Speak, Eira." Death commanded, as was his right being the oldest of all the Sovereigns.

Eira felt all their weight and worked to keep her voice level. "I crossed the veil. More often than our custom. I wore the veil's bounds. I did not command mortal will without reason, nor bind, nor slaughter. I saved a life that would have ended beneath a car's wheel because I am not made to watch a life end within my reach while my hands are empty." She paused, the simple truth steadying her. "And I would do that part again."

Vireth's mouth tilted as he spread his arms wide. "There it is."

"The Law forbids loving a mortal," Fury said. "Not catching one."

"Then ask the question you want," Eira said, tired of their accusations. She wanted it to be out, wanted her siblings to know that she knew and understood her wrong. What she needed was a way to make it right.

It was Sedara who dared it, delighted to be the one. "Do you love him?"

The answer wanted out like light, and Peace, who is truth's oldest friend, had to hold very still.

"I do not know," Eira said softly, and the words were honest enough to wound. "I know only that when he is near, my realm steadies and fractures both. I know the Balance leans. I know the Loom answers when he draws."

Zivael went still, as if realizing exactly what Eira was saying. "He draws?"

"He sees," Eira said. "Threads. Patterns. Fractures. Since childhood. Without language for them. He draws what we look away from when we have looked too long." Her words spread around the circle the way a cold passes through a crowd. Quiet, then sudden, then everywhere. Even Fury's scorn thinned.

"No mortal sees the Loom," Melora said, soft as rain on the lid of a coffin.

"Yet he does," Eira said. "I have seen his hands move with a recognition that is not taught."

Akria turned the ring again, her eyes narrowed. "An anomaly should be cauterized, not cherished."

Zivael's eyes held Eira's as she spoke. "An anomaly is often a sign, not an illness."

"Signs lead armies to cliffs," Vireth said.

Elestra pressed the tips of her fingers together at her lips, lost in thought before speaking. "Or to doors we could not open alone."

Thaloré looked to the center of the chamber. Threads brightened and dimmed with a rhythm none of them controlled. "We are straying," he said. "The question before us is not whether mortals can see. The question is what we will do with Peace."

Fury lifted a gauntleted hand, palm up, as if offering the simplest path. "Bind her to her waters. Thirty cycles. No crossings. Let the mortal's thread take its course. When Balance steadies, release her."

"It will not be enough," Akria said without heat. "When desire is the wound, distance is a tourniquet at best."

Vireth's voice sharpened. "Then make it sufficient. Exile. Prohibition. Censure at the next High Convergence, formal and written, with the Architect's law invoked by name."

Sedara toyed with a lock of hair, smiling. "Or ask a sweeter price. Let her choose, him or her throne." She was enjoying every minute of this torture, and did little to hide it. "What will it be, sister? Pleasure? Or pain." Her smile was cold as she stared pointedly at Eira.

Melora flinched, leveling a steely glare at Sedara. "Do not make love a blade. It cuts even when meant to heal. Eira is still our sister." The last words came firm yet gentle, meant to reassure Eira that not all of her siblings wished her harm.

Lysera reached for the bells at her ankle as if to quiet them. "If you push her away from us, my halls will go quiet altogether."

Elestra's veil trembled with her breath as she agreed with her sister. "Bind her, and my mercy will curdle. Mortals will learn to forgive out of terror. Then it will not be mercy, it will be surrender."

Zivael spoke last among them. "Balance is a law, not a god. It asserts itself because it must. We interfere least when we learn what it asks." She inclined her head toward Eira. "Tell us why you cross, sister, beyond the one life saved. If you want us to be merciful, be specific."

Eira did not mind the demand. Precision was the only kindness left. "Because the mortal world feeds what I am made to be. Not as worship does, not as prayer, for those are for other days. Because sitting among them, hearing the soft quarrel of lovers on a train, watching a baker's shoulders lift when the first loaf rises, feeling a crowd lean toward music in a park...those things are peace moving through bodies. Not stillness, not quiet, but alignment. My realm answers. I cross to remember how peace breathes, because I fear I have forgotten."

That confession settled like warm rain. Even Vireth's fingers paused their tapping.

"And him?" Fury said, voice low, dangerous with the one tenderness he allows himself, rage for a sibling's harm. "What is he, besides an excuse to stand in doorways?"

Eira let herself think of Adrian the way she did when she was alone. The way beauty sat on him like a fact, the way his hand steadied when he drew, the line between his brow when he refused despair.

"He is a place where my stillness learns to move," she said simply. "He is also a danger I chose. I am not innocent in this."

The Loom brightened at that, for honesty pays a tithe to inevitability. Threads wove tighter, binding choice to consequence.

"Enough," Thamys snapped. "We are not poets. This is a trial, and I am bored of it."

He never was one for long winded conversations, and Eira knew he was reaching the end of his patience. She stared at her sibling, noting how he was beautiful in the way a storm is beautiful, terrible and impossible to turn away from.

His features were sharp, refined and regal, but his eyes burned with a violence that made the air seem thinner. Even in stillness, he looked like motion barely contained, the promise of ruin clothed in grace. She was sure she would receive none from him.

Thaloré inclined his head. "Then let it be one." He lifted a strong hand. From the wall, engraved letters uncurled and took the air like silver fish. The Code of the Sovereigns wrote itself above them:

No Direct Alteration of Mortal Will.
Walk Veiled.
Do Not Slay or Bind Another Without Consent.
Respect Domains.
Keep the Balance.

No Sovereign May Love a Mortal.

The last line burned a fraction brighter, as if pleased to be noticed.

"Article Six is clear," Vireth said. "If love is not yet confessed, the slope is greased."

"Article One is equally clear," Elestra returned gently. "She did not compel. She only caught."

"Article Five is the pulse we are hearing," Akria said. "Her balance failed inside her and bled outward."

"The remedy for this?" Death asked. For a moment, every Sovereign's gaze turned to Eira. They went around the circle like a clock with odd hours.

Thamys leaned forward, eyes like hammered bronze narrowing. "Binding to realm" he intoned, the words heavy as iron. "Thirty cycles, renewed on review." His jaw set as though the decree was already carved.

Melora tilted her head, a small smile playing at her lips, pale hair drifting as though stirred by a tide unseen.

"A binding that is also a harbor," she countered softly. "Visitation allowed at dawns only."

Vireth, tall and dark-eyed, spoke without moving more than his lips. His gaze was fixed on some point far beyond the chamber. "No visitation. Cut the thread between them by will, and let both live."

Sedara's laughter rang sharp as broken glass. She reclined in her seat, eyes gleaming with cruel delight. "Let them burn and be done with it. I vote for her to choose mortal or mantle."

Those before her turned sharply in her direction, their brows drawn tight, mouths set in hard lines of disapproval.

Akria, hands clasped behind her, gave a short nod. "Restraint and witness. Appoint one of us to watch her crossings. Pain is information, so I shall gather it."

Lysera's voice was soft but unbroken, her dark eyes reflecting an inner glow. She brushed a strand of silver hair from her face, the gesture delicate. "Give her a vow to keep. Let joy be the measure, and should my halls brighten, her crossings stand but should they dim, she stops."

Elestra pressed a hand to her chest, her veil stirring with the motion. Her voice was soft, barely more than a whisper to those attuned enough to hear. "I offer sponsorship. Let my hands be the threshold she crosses. If harm comes, I will bear it." Then she squared her shoulders, her resolve settling like stone.

Zivael, standing apart, gave a weary shake of her head. "Stay your hands. We are guessing in a dark room. Should we defer to the Fates?" There were several sharp intakes of breath at this.

Eira rose to face her siblings. "A stay," she said. "Not for indulgence. For clarity. If the Loom denies him..." Her words dissolved into silence, for they all knew some endings could not be spoken in that place.

The Loom answered before any Sovereign did. A single thread near the center brightened, silver with a faint green fire in it, and curved across a hum of others. Eira felt it in her chest the way she felt winter reaching for river water.

A second thread, darker and denser, tilted toward the first and then away, like two bodies recognizing and refusing in a single motion. Between them, the smallest of knots acknowledged itself, no more than a thought becoming a word. No one spoke. Even Sedara sat upright.

When the glow faded, Thaloré stood. "We defer," he said, and it was as close to reverence as he used. "By custom and wisdom, when the Loom moves before we do, we do not stampede."

Fury's jaw worked. "Defer how long?"

"Until the next quieting of Balance," Death said. "The cycle of a moon. In that time, Peace will submit to conditions."

Vireth's mouth curved, satisfied by the word submit. "Name them."

Death did not hesitate. "Veil intact at all times among mortals.

No alteration of mortal will, beyond the catching of falling bodies and the staying of imminent death by accident." His eyes lifted to Eira. "No crossings at moments of large assembly, where ripples multiply. No speech of who she is. If fights break around her, she departs. If a place goes preternaturally still, she departs. If Mercy's hands tremble or Joy's bells dull in the hour after she returns, the stay is revoked."

Elestra lifted her veil's edge enough for breath. "I will make the threshold," she said, standing. "Let her pass by me each time. If her crossings harm, I will feel it first."

Akria inclined her head. "I will witness," she said.

Sedara's smile returned, lazy as a cats. "And I will keep my sweets to myself, for once." She flicked a hand. "Let the trial be done. It's becoming more trouble than it's worth."

Zivael glanced around the circle. "Then it is a covenant, not a cage."

Fury's cloak hissed across the floor when he turned away. "One moon," he growled. "If the world sours further, I will not be talked into patience again."

Melora watched Eira with eyes like deep wells. "If you love him," she said very softly when the others moved, "teach your love not to shatter what it holds."

Alone with the Loom's hum and the sound of departing footsteps, Eira stood very still. Her hands had not unclenched. She felt the conditions settle on her like a mantle cut to fit- bearable, heavy, exact.

Thaloré paused beside her before he vanished to his river. "Peace," he said without chill or pity. "In the mortal realm, there is a difference between holding and clinging. Learn it quickly."

He left her in the great round hall with the arches looking out on every weather. When she finally sat, the obsidian floor held her reflection without a ripple. She let her shoulders drop the least amount a goddess could and breathed until the breath moved through her hands.

The moon glowed overhead, the Code written in light before sinking once more into stone. A stay murmured the knot where two threads crossed. Eira stood. Her gown shimmered white in the chamber's pale fire, and as she turned away, she let herself imagine for a single, reckless heartbeat the lamp with its dented shade, the mugs staining, the unfinished eyes on the canvas she would not let him paint. She put the thought down the way one sets a cup carefully on a sill and stepped into the veil without disturbing the surface.

Behind her, the Convergence chamber exhaled. Out beyond its arches, storms kept their manners, rivers remembered their banks, and somewhere in a city that would never know this room existed a kettle clicked alive at the exact moment a fight at the corner bar dissolved into apologies no one expected to accept.

For Eira, the answer had always been there, like a thread drawn taut through her soul. She knew what she must do, though every law screamed against it. There was only one path left, and she would follow it until the end unraveled. If love was not worth fighting for, then nothing in all the realms ever could be.

CHAPTER 9
EIRA

The veil parted with less resistance than it should have. That alone was enough to trouble her. Eira felt it in her bones, a loosening of the world's fabric where there should have been taut strength. Passing into the mortal realm no longer required the stilling of her breath or the careful dimming of her essence. The world had grown accustomed to her presence, and that was dangerous. Yet she stepped through anyway.

The city's air pressed against her with warmth and grit, rich with smoke from street carts and the sharp tang of rain still clinging to the stones. Eira drew her coat tighter, though she never truly felt the chill and had no need for it. The fabric smelled faintly of Adrian, oil paint, honey, and rain. The reprieve had begun. A stay, one cycle long, granted by her siblings and Balance itself. She had sworn to be careful. She had sworn to cross lightly. But tonight she had no intention of leaving quickly.

Adrian was waiting. She found him at his easel, the lamplight turning his skin to bronze, the fall of his dark hair shadowing the strong line of his jaw. His shirt hung loose at the collar, sleeves rolled past his elbows, smudges of green paint staining his wrist. The brush moved in sure strokes, but his attention was elsewhere. His body was in the room; his thoughts reached beyond.

Eira stood in the doorway longer than she meant to, her hands clasped at her waist, watching him work. The figure on the canvas was hers again, white dress flowing, the auburn hair imagined into being, the form luminous against shadow. He had caught something of her essence without ever seeing her whole. Always he stopped at the eyes.

Adrian spoke without turning. "You linger."

Her lips curved faintly. "And you knew I was here."

Her delicate lips widened into a smile that she tried to suppress. But what was she suppressing, really? This fragile, mortal man could stop her heart with a smile. She couldn't hide that from herself anymore, not really, if she were honest with herself.

Adrian set the brush aside, rising from the stool. When he turned, his eyes, dark pools catching lamplight, caught her and held. "I always do. I always will."

For a moment she said nothing. The world narrowed to the sound of rain dripping from the eaves, the faint buzz of the lamp, the rough warmth of his presence. She should have returned at once, before the ripple grew. Instead, she stepped inside and let the door close.

THEY WALKED TOGETHER through the night streets, her coat trailing just a little too long, his stride easy beside hers. The market was still awake, lanterns strung across stalls, vendors calling out, scents of cumin and roasted meat thick in the air. Adrian bought figs, pressing one into her hand.

"Try this," he urged.

The fruit split beneath her fingers, red as a wound, sweet as fire when she tasted it. She laughed, surprised, and the sound startled her as much as him. It had been too long since laughter left her throat so easily.

"Better than tea?" Adrian asked, grinning.

"Different," she said, licking juice from her lip. "But I think I like it."

They lingered at a flower stand, daisies nodding in the lamplight. The vendor pressed a handful into her arms, and Adrian paid without hesitation. She held them carefully, but already the stems bent, the petals bowing toward her. Her presence weighted them. Mortals would see only wilt, but Adrian saw more. He always saw more. His brow furrowed but he said nothing, only walked beside her as though nothing at all was strange.

As they walked, their hands touched, and found themselves intertwined. The air grew heavier, and Adrian felt a weight lift itself off of his chest. This moment was a million moments wrapped in one, and his heart threatened to burst from the happiness he was experiencing.

The park was slick with rain, lamps glimmering against wet stone. A guitarist played beneath an awning, notes thin but true. Children darted between benches, laughter echoing, their shoes splashing puddles. Couples leaned into one another, sharing umbrellas.

Eira slowed, taking everything in. This was peace in its mortal form, not silence, not still water, but the balancing of discord into harmony. Voices overlapping, laughter breaking against sorrow, life pressing forward despite itself. She had never understood it that way until she walked the mortal realm at that moment.

Adrian glanced at her, awestruck, then looked down at their hands that were still intertwined as they walked.

"You look like you belong." He left out *with me.*

Her throat tightened. "I never do."

Adrian didn't press, or fill the quietness with words. But his gaze lingered, steady and searching. Before he could reply, she leaned up and kissed him slowly. The passion of a thousand suns burned between them, latching on to everything she ever was and ever would be. It was not hurried, not desperate, but something slower, a testing of fragile ground. His breath caught against hers and he kissed her back, greedy and gentle at the same time.

His hands caressed her neck, the other roaming freely throughout her tresses. She felt something within him call to her, and she opened her very essence to answer. *I am yours*, it said. She repeated the words aloud, as he caressed the side of her face, his lips never leaving hers. When she drew away, her pulse unsteady, the wind brushed her lips like an afterthought.

Adrian's voice stayed low. "You do belong. More than you think."

At that moment, he knew. He knew that what he felt for Eira was more than curiosity, more than intrigue. Some part of him had known since the moment he first laid eyes on her. He had never known the feeling of falling in love, but this? There were no words for how he felt for Eira. He would sell his soul to the highest bidder for more stolen moments with her.

In that moment, something in the universe gave way, quietly, irrevocably. And it began. Two men argued, their shouts slicing through the quiet. A crowd gathered quickly, drawn to the heat of it. One shoved, the other struck back, and suddenly fists were flying, voices raised, bodies colliding. Adrian moved, but Eira stepped forward first. She lifted her hand, not touching, only releasing the smallest breath of her essence, letting power flow through her.

The air went still. The men froze mid-strike. Their anger dissolved, replaced by confusion, shame. They stumbled back, blinking at one another as if waking from a dream. The crowd murmured, uncertain, then drifted apart. Lightning struck in every direction, tearing across the sky, and the ground trembled beneath them as though something vast and ancient were about to rise.

Adrian's eyes fixed on her, and she could see the worry in them. "Was that you?"

Before she could answer, the lamp above the fountain burst, raining glass. The guitarist's strings snapped with a shriek. Children began to cry. Eira flinched. Balance pressed against her chest, heavy, unseen.

"Come now, we must leave," she whispered, and they left the park behind.

The city grew worse as they walked. On one street, silence fell too suddenly. Cars halted mid- intersection, drivers staring blankly through their windshields. A woman dropped her purse, coins scattering, and stood motionless, tears sliding down her cheeks for no reason. At the next corner, the opposite: laughter erupted, wild and uncontrolled. Strangers clutched one another, gasping until their bodies shook, collapsing against lampposts with tears in their eyes. It wasn't joy. It was hysteria.

Adrian caught her hand, his grip urgent. "Eira, what is happening?"

Her pulse hammered, and her words spilled quickly. "The world notices me. I shouldn't have come, but I wanted to see you one last time... This is my fault. I may have doomed us all!"

Confusion etched the lines of his beautiful face, but there was no time for questions, no room for demands. "Then let me be doomed with you," he whispered.

By the time they reached his apartment, her strength faltered. The kettle screamed in the kitchen though no flame touched it. The lamp flickered violently, shadows jumping against the walls. Outside, a fight broke out in the alley, voices raw with rage, then dissolved seconds later into sobbing embraces.

Eira sank onto the rug, pressing her hands into her lap to quiet their trembling. Adrian knelt in front of her, hair falling loose, eyes locked on hers as he caressed her cheek.

"You can't keep this inside anymore. Strange things are happening, and I don't know how to help or what to do! You're always speaking of endings, always saying you shouldn't see me. And I know what I saw. I need you to tell me. Tell me, Eira." He moved closer, placing his hands on either side of her face until his breath brushed her skin. "Please, tell me what you are." His voice carried urgency, but beneath it she heard the deeper fear of losing her.

Her throat tightened. Words fought against silence, forbidden and dangerous. She lowered her eyes. "If I do, you will not thank me. It will *doom* us, Adrian."

"I will not lose you," he said desperately, clutching her as though she might vanish between one breath and the next.

She raised her gaze and let out a long exhale, the sound soft but threaded with resolve. For one heartbeat she let the veil slip, her eyes burning gold-green, her golden essence seeping through her glamour and the room seemed to pause, suspended in a silence that vibrated with power.

Adrian's breath caught. Words failed him in the face of what she had revealed. All he wanted to do was fall at her feet, to worship her, to love her with everything he was. Too many feelings warred within him, each pulling him apart. His hand rose, trembled with the weight of choice, then faltered and fell uselessly to his side.

The lamp shattered. Outside, sirens screamed. Eira gasped, clutching her chest. Balance had felt her breach. Adrian caught her as she staggered. His arms held her tight, his voice fierce against her ear.

"Eira! What can I do?" His voice cracked with panic. His arms closed around her, holding her as if he could shield her from everything beyond his grasp. He pressed a fierce kiss to her forehead. "We're going home. I'll protect you. Nothing will harm you. I'll never let *anything* harm you!"

She closed her eyes, pressing her face into his shoulder and let herself cling, as the world unraveled around them.

Above, unseen, the Loom shivered. Two threads bent close and touched for the briefest instant. A choice was sealed, their fates entwined. A knot sparked into being, and the Weavers' hands went still. The scissors gleamed, and Balance waited.

CHAPTER 10
EIRA

When they arrived at Adrian's apartment, he found glass scattered across the rug, glittering in the lamplight. His hand was firm on her shoulder, steadying her as though his mortal touch could hold back Balance itself. Eira leaned into him, desperate for that anchor, when the air shifted.

The silence came first. Not the silence she commanded, the hush of rivers and dawn breezes, but a suffocating stillness that devoured the edges of sound. The city outside ceased its noise. The whistle of the kettle cut short. Even Adrian's breath stalled against her ear. Then the shadows rose.

They crawled along the corners of the room, blackening the walls, swallowing the lamplight. Eira's eyes widened as the darkness thickened and folded in upon itself. Adrian's grip tightened. "Eira," he whispered, and there was fear in it now, sharp and helpless.

Her heart jolted. "No, not yet-"

The shadows surged upward. They wrapped her like cold smoke, winding around her arms, her waist, her throat. She reached for Adrian, fingers brushing his hand, but in an instant the world yawned open beneath her. His face vanished, his voice torn away. The darkness swallowed her whole. It pressed against her skin, weightless and crushing at once.

She fell without falling, her body suspended in cold air that carried no breath. The scent of stone and river water seeped in. The shadows thinned, and when she opened her eyes she was standing on polished marble in Thaloré's hall.

The vast chamber spread out beneath a ceiling that did not exist. Mist hung above, endless and shifting, broken only by a faint pale glow. Beside her ran the river, wide and black, its surface glinting with ghostly light as souls drifted in the current. They whispered as they passed, voices soft as the sigh of wind through graves.

Thaloré stood at the river's edge. He did not need to announce himself. He was the stillness of the chamber, the pause in the river's breath. His robes, black as the void, were stitched with constellations, each star faintly burning. A circlet of bone crowned his dark hair. His eyes, pale as river mist, found her where she stood.

"Peace." His voice was solemn, filled with judgment. Her knees wanted to buckle, but she forced herself upright, fingers trembling at her sides.

"You had no right," she shouted, though her voice came out thin. The shadows stirred at his feet. At a gesture from his hand, they wound up from the floor and coiled around her wrists, her ankles, her waist. They did not hurt, not yet, but the cold was deep enough to silence her breath.

"You would lecture me on rights?" His voice was low, resonant, like the toll of a funeral bell. "You, who unravel Balance with every breath in the mortal world?"

"I have harmed no one," she whispered.

His eyes narrowed. He extended his hand toward the river. Eira turned. And her breath caught. The souls drifted wrong. Some tore through too quickly, snatched from bodies that still should have lived. She saw them thrash as they entered the current, confusion and fear clinging. Others lingered at the edge, refusing to cross, clinging to invisible threads with unnatural tenacity. The river stuttered, faltering like a failing heart.

"This is you," Thaloré said. The shadows at her throat tightened faintly with his words. "A child died three days too soon. An old man clings in agony, his thread refusing to sever. Soldiers swing their swords with hesitation, or with rage sharpened beyond their cause. Death does not do this. Balance does not do this. Discord does. Is that what you will ascend to, dear sister?" His tone was sharp, accusing.

Eira's chest heaved. "I never meant for-"

"Meaning." His voice sliced through her, silencing her words. "Meaning does not matter. Law does." He stepped closer. His robe stirred the mist. The weight of him filled the chamber.

"Tell me, sister. Will you keep breaking the world for the love of a mortal? Or will you let him go?"

The shadows pressed closer. She could feel their chill seep into her bones.

"I cannot," she said, her voice cracking.

For the first time, something flickered in his pale eyes. Not softness, never that, but recognition.

He tilted his head. "Then you will not be given the choice much longer."

The river roared, louder now. The souls' whispers rose into a wail that echoed through the mist. And in that sound she heard Adrian's voice, his breath cut off as she was torn away, his hand reaching. She clutched the memory like a weapon against the cold, her tears falling silently to the marble floor.

The shadows shifted beneath her feet. At Thaloré's gesture, the coils around her wrists loosened enough for her to move, though they clung still, reminding her that she was not free. He turned without a word, his long robe trailing mist, and began to walk along the river's edge.

"Come," he said, his voice commanding.

She wanted to resist. Every part of her longed to tear free and return across the veil, back to Adrian's warmth, back to the mortal world where she could pretend for a little longer. But the shadows tightened when she lingered, dragging her forward until her steps fell into rhythm with his.

The river whispered louder as they walked. Shapes drifted in the current- pale, translucent, glowing faintly like starlight caught in water. Some were still, their eyes closed, drifting in silence. Others writhed, clawing toward the surface, mouths opening in noiseless screams.

Thaloré stopped at the body of a child. The soul was small, its glow fragile, its features blurred but unmistakably young. It clutched a ragged thread that trailed back toward the mist, a thread that had been cut too soon.

"This boy," Thaloré said, his pale eyes fixed on her. "He should have lived three more days. He would have spoken a word his mother longed to hear. He would have changed her grief into strength. Instead, the Balance tilted, and a wheel turned at the wrong time. His breath ended."

Eira's throat closed. She pressed her hand to her lips as tears spilled down her face. "No…"

Thaloré's gaze did not waver. "You did this, Eira. Your presence in the mortal realm pulled threads that should not yet have crossed."

The shadows urged her forward. They passed a man lying half in, half out of the current. His body glowed faintly, but his eyes were open, wide, staring. His soul strained backward, refusing to sink fully into the river.

"This one lingers," Thaloré said quietly, sadness threading through his words. "He was meant to pass, his thread cut clean. But Balance faltered, and he clings still. His body decays. His family weeps over him, praying for release that does not come."

Eira felt her knees weaken. "Release him, Thaloré. I did not know this would be the price, please- "

"I cannot." Thaloré's voice was quiet but final. "Until the thread yields, even Death waits. And threads obey Balance. It is your hand that has tangled them."

The shadows pushed her onward. They came to a cluster of souls drifting together, their forms blurred but restless. Beyond them she glimpsed the images of soldiers locked in battle. Their blades wavered. One struck with sudden rage, his blow cleaving deeper than it should. Another faltered, lowering his weapon, cut down in hesitation.

"War," Thaloré said. "A thousand threads cross here. Some fray too quickly, others delay. Men die when they should have lived. Others live when their time is done. Every hesitation, every excess stroke, ripples outward. And when the war ends, their descendants will live in a world unbalanced."

Eira's tears slid down her cheeks, hot against the cold shadows. She shook her head, words splintering on her tongue.

"I only wanted-" she began, but the words were cut short.

"You wanted him," Thaloré snapped, turning on her. The shadows surged higher, tightening around her chest, her throat. His voice was low thunder, stripped of pity. "And in wanting, you tore what should not tear."

She gasped, fighting the weight pressing against her lungs. "He sees the Loom!" she cried, desperate for her brother to understand. "He sees their threads as no mortal should. It cannot be accident. He is meant to- I don't know- he is DESTINED for-"

"Meant?" Death's voice cut her to the bone, cold and harsh. "Do not speak of what is meant. Not to me. I am the ending of all meanings."

The shadows constricted until she could not breathe. The souls in the river keened, their whispers rising into wails. For a moment she thought he would crush her there, let her dissolve into his mist and never return. But then, as suddenly as they had seized her, the shadows loosened. She staggered, falling to her knees on the cold marble, her breath tearing in and out.

Thaloré loomed above her, his pale eyes unreadable. "Do not mistake the moon's reprieve as mercy. It is only Balance's patience. When it ends, either you will break from him, or the world will break from you."

The shadows withdrew fully, seeping back into the stones. The river quieted, though the souls still whispered, restless and wrong. Eira knelt there, trembling, her tears falling into the marble until they vanished like they had never been. Her heart burned with grief, with defiance, with fear. And above the river, faint but undeniable, the Loom shimmered. Threads gleamed gold and black, twining together. The knot pulsed once, bright as a heartbeat. Thaloré's gaze flicked to it, then back to her. For the first time, something like doubt shadowed his face.

"You are playing with inevitability, sister," he said, and Eira heard the sadness in his voice. "And inevitability always wins."

The hall dimmed around her, and with a single blink the marble, the river, and the mist dissolved. He was gone, and the weight of the mortal realm closed in around her once more.

Eira blinked Adrian's apartment into view, looking around confused. The kettle lay silent, shattered glass at her feet, Adrian standing frozen in the lamplight with fear carved across his face. His hands shook as he reached for her.

"Eira! What happened?" His voice shook, raw with worry.

She swallowed hard, her voice laced with sadness.

"Everything," she whispered. "And nothing you can bear to know."

Her heart still felt the weight of the shadows, and the wails of the river still clung to her ears. Throwing caution to the wind, she dared say aloud the words that she couldn't let her mouth speak earlier.

"Adrian," she whispered tenderly, meeting his eyes, "I love you. And it is going to be the end of me. But it's better I say it now because I might not have the chance to say it again."

This time, she felt Balance disrupt around her.

CHAPTER II
EIRA

The veil had never felt so thick. For three nights Eira did not return to the mortal world. Each time she drew near, each time Adrian's thread glimmered in the Loom like a star calling to her, she faltered. The memory of Thaloré's hand, of shadows strangling her breath, of the souls writhing in his rivers were too much for her to carry into his presence. To look upon Adrian's face would undo her, especially after her confession. So she drifted instead.

She walked the spaces between realms where no mortal eye had ever lingered. The high ridges of mountains whose names had been lost before the first empire rose, where snow lay endless and blue under a sky brittle with stars. She sat on the ice-capped peak, the wind lashing her auburn hair about her face, her white gown pressed close to her skin. The world below was silent, untouched.

Here, no protests shook the streets, no laughter rose wild, no trace of human presence at all. Only stone, ice, and air. She folded her arms about her knees and let her forehead rest against them. *What had she done?*

Eira could not stop the flood of memories from Thaloré's realm.

The boy's soul, ripped too soon from his body. The old man clinging at the edge of the river. The soldiers, their swords cutting deeper than fate decreed. Thaloré's words echoed in her chest, sharp as a blade to the core. *"This is you."* She could not deny it. The truth was hers, and so was the disruption she had unleashed.

She told herself she had meant no harm. That her desire was not violence, only love. But even love could unmake the world if it disobeyed the Law. The veil shimmered faintly at the edge of her vision, threads trembling as though Balance itself waited for her to decide. She closed her eyes and turned away. When she could bear her solitude no longer, she sought her sister.

Sorrow's realm was always dim, a twilight place where the sky wept a gentle rain and the air smelled faintly of salt. Rivers wandered through it, slow and deep, lined with black willows whose roots drank the tears of the world. Where she walked, flowers of blue and violet bloomed briefly before bowing their heads and fading back into the soil.

Eira stepped into that soft gloom with relief. Here, sorrow was not shame but sanctuary. Here, her trembling heart was allowed to ache. Melora sat by the edge of a quiet pool, her indigo gown spread about her like a mourning veil, her long black hair streaked with silver falling loose down her back. Her eyes lifted when Eira entered, deep and endless, and in them was no judgment, only recognition.

"You have come at last," Melora said, her voice low, weighted like rain falling steadily on stone.

Eira sank down beside her, folding her white gown about her knees. "You felt it."

"I feel everything." Melora reached out, trailing her fingers across the water.

Ripples spread, catching faint reflections of countless grieving faces. Mothers, widows, children, and soldiers. They faded as quickly as they appeared.

"But yours most keenly. You do not weep often, sister. When you do, the world trembles." Melora's voice was soft, her gaze resting tenderly on her sister.

Eira bowed her head. "Thaloré showed me. The child. The old man. The souls. I thought I could carry it, but-" Her voice broke. "It is too much."

Melora's hand slipped into hers, cool and soft, the press of silver rings gentle against Eira's skin. "You love him." The words carried no judgment, only truth.

Eira's eyes fell shut, the truth rising from her soul before she could stop it. "Yes."

"And you hate yourself for it." Melora continued.

"Yes." Was all Eira could bring herself to reply.

Melora's gaze returned to the pool, watching the shifting faces. "Then you are not alone. Sorrow is born from love as often as from cruelty. You are living both."

Eira looked at her sister, her chest aching. "Tell me what to do."

Melora smiled faintly, and it was the saddest smile in the world. "I am not Truth. I cannot show you the path. I can only sit with you in the ache until you choose it."

The rain thickened, pattering softly against their hair and gowns, sliding down their cheeks like tears neither had to shed. For the first time in days, Eira let herself lean. Her head rested against Melora's shoulder, her tears mingling with the rain, and her sister held her hand and asked nothing more.

The rain in Sorrow's realm thickened as Eira leaned against her sister's shoulder, but it was a gentle rain, one that washed rather than punished. They sat together in silence, the hush of falling water wrapping them like a shroud.

At last, Melora stirred. She drew her hand from Eira's and let her fingers trail across the surface of the pool again. Ripples spread, and for a moment a face rose there, the shadow of a young man, his eyes dark, his mouth curved in laughter Eira could not hear.

"You think you are the first," Melora said softly. "But you are not."

Eira turned her head, searching her sister's beautiful pale face in confusion. "You loved a mortal?"

The corners of Melora's lips curved faintly, but the smile was too heavy to last. "Once. Long ago, when empires were still young, and the world had not yet learned the full cruelty of men. His name was Callen. He was a singer." The rain dimmed, as though the sky itself leaned closer to hear.

"He sang not for crowds, not for kings," Melora continued, her gaze distant. "He sang to mourners in the fields, to mothers who buried their sons, to lovers who laid flowers on graves. His voice was grief made beautiful, and I-I could not look away. I lingered longer than I should have, listening. I told myself I was only easing his burden, guiding his sorrow into mine. But the truth..." She pressed her palm flat against her chest. "The truth was that I loved him."

Eira's throat tightened. "What happened?"

Melora's eyes dropped back to the pool. The man's face dissolved into ripples, his features lost.

"At first, nothing. He lived, he sang, I listened. But the world does not forgive what we are. My presence lengthened his grief. The mourners who came to him stayed longer in their sorrow. Fields went untended, wars dragged on, children grew in houses shadowed by mourning. Balance bent. And then..." Melora's voice caught. She closed her eyes. "Then Callen saw me. Truly saw me. He thought I was a dream, a spirit come to ease his song. He sang for me, and in his voice was devotion so fierce the Loom itself trembled. It cut his thread that night. His heart stopped as he sang, and he fell with my name on his lips."

The pool stilled utterly, the rain vanishing into silence. Eira's tears mingled with the wetness of her sister's gown.

"Melora, I'm so sorry," she whispered, wanting to ease this pain from her kindest sister.

Sorrow turned her gaze upon her, those endless eyes brimming with the weight of a thousand griefs. "I do not speak to burden you, but to warn you," Melora said, her voice low, her gaze lost to the distance. "Love is not forbidden for its weakness. It is forbidden for its strength. Even Peace cannot withstand the unraveling it brings."

Eira bowed her head into her sister's shoulder, grief shaking her. "But what am I, if not Peace? What worth is my realm if I cannot even hold the one thing I was made to preserve?"

Melora's hand stroked her hair gently, as a mother might soothe a child. "You are not broken for wanting him. You are only breaking because you believe you can keep him without cost."

The rain returned, heavier now, pattering like a thousand soft tears on stone. For a long while, they sat together, the goddess of Peace and the goddess of Sorrow, their gowns soaking, their tears indistinguishable from the rain.

At last Melora whispered, "If you choose him, do not pretend it will be easy. And if you leave him, do not pretend it will be gentle. Either way, sister, you will grieve. The only choice is what kind of grief you are willing to bear."

Eira closed her eyes, her heart breaking open beneath the words. She saw Adrian's face in her mind, the warmth of his smile, the darkness of his eyes. She saw the shattered glass, the violent mortals, the souls in Thaloré's river. She saw the knot flickering in the Loom, brighter each day. She did not answer. She could not. But in her silence, Melora held her hand tighter, and for a little while Eira let herself believe that even grief could be endured when shared.

CHAPTER 12
EIRA

The mountain winds had stripped her of excuses. Melora's warning had broken her heart, but in the days that followed, Eira felt something stronger rise in its place. Desire, yes, but braided with defiance. She did not want to let him go. Not Adrian, with his dark eyes like midnight pools, his hands steady at the canvas, his laughter too rare but all the brighter for it. Not the mortal who had looked at her veil of stillness and called it beautiful instead of empty.

She had tasted centuries of obedience to the Law, and she found she no longer cared to bend her neck. But love alone was not enough. Not when the world trembled at her crossing. Not when Balance snarled at her heels. So she turned her thoughts toward answers.

Adrian should not see the threads. No mortal could. Yet he drew them as though they had always lived in his hands. She remembered the sketches scattered across his desk, lines twisting, weaving, crossing, forming shapes that should not exist in a mind untouched by the Loom. He should not know them. And yet he did. There had to be a reason.

Eira began to walk the hidden places of the realms. She drifted through the caverns where the Architect's name was still etched into stone, half-erased by time. She lingered at the edges of the Loom itself, watching the Fates' silent hands move. Always she searched for clues, for whispers, for some forgotten story that explained him.

In one hall of broken pillars, she found carvings of mortals standing beneath Sovereigns, their eyes upturned, their hands raised. But among them was one figure set apart, his eyes wide with light, a thread wound between his fingers. The inscription was ancient, its language older than most tongues, but she understood enough. Seers of the Thread. A lineage so rare it had been lost to memory. Her heart quickened. Was Adrian one of them?

Eira traced the carving with her fingertips. The figure's face was worn away by centuries, but the thread in his hands glimmered faintly, a residue of Balance itself. The wind howled through the broken hall.

Eira pressed her palm flat against the stone, whispering, "Tell me why him." The stone gave no answer. But the air shifted, and the Loom's hum filled her ears.

Back in the mortal world, she began to notice more. When Adrian slept, his breath grew uneven, his hands twitching as though he sketched even in dreams. She saw the faint shimmer of threads around his head, weaving into his dreams like silver vines. Once, he woke with tears on his cheeks, whispering words he did not remember in the morning. Each sign sharpened her conviction. If he was a Seer of the Thread, then perhaps his bond with her was not a transgression but a design.

Perhaps Balance had given her this mortal, not to break her, but to change what had always been. Yet the risk remained a threat. If she loved him openly, the Fates would make her mortal or destroy her. If she clung too tightly, Balance would rip the world apart. But what if there was another way?

Sitting in his apartment while he painted, she let her eyes linger on the unfinished canvases. Always her image, always her eyes blank, as if he waited for her to allow the truth to be drawn. She touched the edge of one canvas lightly, her voice no louder than breath.

"I will find a way," she whispered.

The lamp flickered, but did not break. The kettle hissed, but softly, almost like a sigh. For the first time since she had crossed into his life, Balance did not roar. It only watched.

Eira had searched the ruins for days. The hall of broken pillars was still cold beneath her feet, the stone inscriptions worn and near forgotten. The figure etched in the wall haunted her. She looked upon the mortal with threads wound between his fingers. She had traced the grooves until her skin burned with the memory of them. Still the carving yielded nothing.

Tonight she sat in silence atop the shattered steps, her white gown damp with the mist curling through the ruins. Adrian's name pulsed in her chest like a wound, and with it the question of why it had to be him, the one mortal she dared to love. She might've asked this aloud, but there was no one there to hear her.

"You will not find the answer by staring at stone." The voice broke the silence. It was low, ancient, threaded with dry amusement.

Eira spun, her hair whipping with the movement. Shadows shifted at the edge of the hall as a figure emerged. At first, Eira thought it was one of her siblings-tall, cloaked, ageless. But as the figure drew closer, she saw the truth; this one bore no sovereign's mark. His robe was tattered, edges unraveling, the fabric caught between light and dark as though it could not decide which realm claimed it. His face was long, lined with centuries, his eyes pale but not lifeless.

"Who are you?" Eira demanded, the authority in her voice rising, reverberating as though the air itself bent to her will. The figure in the shadows stilled, caught between defiance and submission, as if deciding whether to answer or to vanish back into the dark.

The figure inclined his head. "A Watcher. Once, long ago, I served the Loom. I carried the records of threads not yet woven." His mouth curved faintly. "Until I asked too many questions."

Eira's pulse quickened. She stepped closer despite herself. "You knew the Seers of the Thread."

The Watcher's eyes sharpened, catching a glint of the dim light. "So you've found their mark." He glanced at the carving on the wall. "Few remember them. Fewer still believe."

"Adrian sees the threads," Eira whispered. "He draws them. He dreams about them. It cannot be by chance."

The Watcher studied her, his gaze old enough to strip pretense. "No. Not by chance. The Seers were born rarely, once in many generations. Mortals with the sight to glimpse what even Sovereigns fear to touch. They were meant to witness. To remind the world that the threads bind all, gods and mortals alike."

Eira's breath caught. "Then he is chosen."

The Watcher's lips thinned. "He is something else entirely. Cursed in the mortal realm, perhaps."

The word cut her. She pressed her hand to her chest, as though steadying herself. "No. He- he is gentle, kind. His gift does not break him."

"Not yet." The Watcher stepped closer, his presence heavy as old stone. "But no mortal should bear the sight for long. It frays the mind, unravels the body. That is why the Seers vanished. The Loom uses them, then ends them. Their threads are never long."

Eira's knees weakened. She gripped the broken pillar beside her, her voice raw. "You mean he will die."

The Watcher tilted his head. "All mortals do. But Seers burn faster. His thread glows bright even now, tangled in yours. The more you linger, the shorter it grows."

Tears stung her eyes. She shook her head violently. "No. There must be a way to save him. To save *us*."

The Watcher's expression softened. not with pity, but recognition. "That is why you searched. That is why you stand in ruins speaking to ghosts. You think love will change what was written."

Eira's voice hardened. "I will find a way."

He regarded her for a long time, then nodded slowly. "Perhaps. But you must understand that to keep him, you must change not just your fate, but the Law. You must ask questions even the Fates do not answer."

His words chilled her. The Fates never spoke. They only cut. Still, something within her flared. Hope and defiance, sharper now, no longer cloaked in grief. She drew herself to her full height and said, with fierce determination, "Then I will go to them."

The Watcher's pale eyes gleamed faintly. "Be careful, daughter of stillness. The Loom does not suffer trespass. To stand before it is to risk being cut yourself."

"I would risk it a thousand times," Eira whispered, "before I lose him once."

The Watcher's faint smile returned, sad and knowing. "Then the world will tremble before you are done."

He turned, his tattered robe dissolving into mist, until only the echo of his words remained.

Eira stood alone in the ruins, her tears cooling on her cheeks, her fists clenched tight at her sides. Above her, the Loom's hum stirred faintly, threads quivering like the strings of a harp. She lifted her gaze, her heart steadying into resolve. If the Law itself was the chain, then she would walk into the hands that forged it. She would find The Fates.

CHAPTER 13

EIRA

The Gates of the Loom rose like a dream from which no waking could come. Not iron, not stone, but living light held their form, threads woven into a lattice of forgotten colors. Gold throbbed like a heartbeat, silver wound through it, whispering with hidden voices. Crimson coiled like fire wrapped in silk, climbing ever higher. Their glow was otherworldly and ancient, older than creation's first breath. And above, spanning the cosmos without end, the Threads of Fate stretched on. They wound and twisted upward, weaving a tapestry that became the sky, and a sky that became eternity.

Eira stopped at the threshold, her breath catching in her throat. This place was revered by all who had stood witness when the Architect began his creation, and avoided by all but the most desperate. She stood in awe of the Gates, struck by their terrible beauty. They called to her, not as her siblings' domains did, but as the sea calls to one who drowns. Her hands curled into fists at her sides. She had come to demand answers, and already the threads were tugging at her, curious which part of her to unravel first.

"Beautiful, isn't it?" The voice drifted down like silk in the wind.

Another voice followed, dry and sharp. "Beautiful, yes, but excessive. Always weaving and weaving. They should have stopped three thousand years ago."

A third sighed, her voice high pitched and lovely. "Solenne, you've complained about the decor since the Flood. Let it go."

The threads stirred, loosening and twining until three figures stood where none had been a moment before. They were tall, robed in flowing cloth that shimmered like constellations, their hair falling in silver, in black, in pale gold. Their faces were the same and not the same, eyes polished glass reflecting strands of fate. They were beautiful and terrible to look upon. The Fates. The Threaded Three. The Silent Loom given voice.

Eira's pulse thundered. She dropped to one knee out of instinct, her voice breaking the silence. "I seek your judgment."

The silver-haired one tilted her head, lips curving. "Judgment? My dear, we hardly have time for all the judgment people want. You'll have to be more specific."

The golden-haired one leaned against the Gates as if they were no more than a garden wall. "Oh, don't tease. She looks terrified enough. Let her speak before she faints."

The black-haired one chuckled softly, low and warm as dark wine. "She will not faint. She has walked here, and none who reach the Gates by will are weak."

Eira raised her head, her voice trembling but clear. "You know why I've come."

"Yes," they said together, three voices woven into one. The Gates shivered with the sound.

Eira steadied herself, forcing her voice to remain strong. "The mortal, Adrian. He sees the threads. He draws them. He dreams them. Why?"

The three exchanged glances, as though amused by the question.

Silver-haired Solenne rolled her eyes. "Always the same question.

'*Why him? Why me? Why now?*' Do you know how many gods and mortals have asked us that?"

"Too many," said Virelith, the black-haired one.

She smiled faintly, almost kindly. "But hers carries weight. Peace rarely asks for herself."

Eira's nails dug into her palms, barely containing her rage. "Then answer me."

The golden- haired one known as Umbra, laughed softly. "Careful, little dove. Demands sound less charming than you think."

The Gates stirred, threads humming like a plucked harp and a vision shimmered before Eira's eyes. Adrian was standing in his apartment, brush in hand, painting her. Then the vision fractured, contorting to show Adrian broken by madness, scratching threads on the walls until his fingers bled. Another fracture, and Adrian was lying still, his thread cut too soon, lips parted in silence. Another-Adrian crowned in light, a leader whose voice swayed thousands.

Eira gasped, clutching her chest. "What is this?"

The silver haired Fate, Solenne, stepped closer, her expression cool. "This is what you ask. You want to know what becomes of him? We show you the truths that may yet be. He is a Seer, yes. He was born to glimpse what should remain veiled. That sight can make him a prophet, or a madman, or a corpse."

Eira's tears stung. "Then help me. Tell me how to keep him from breaking!"

Umbra tilted her head, eyes glinting with mischief. "Keep him? You already know the Law. You cannot love him without unraveling yourself and worse, unraveling him."

"Unless," Virelith murmured, her voice like velvet over a blade, "you change the Law itself."

The others fell silent. Even the Gates hushed. Eira's heart pounded.

"Change...the Law?" Solenne arched a brow. "Oh, that's bold. Naïve, but bold."

Umbra's lips curved into a slow smile. "You'd have to weave a new thread into the Code itself. Rewrite what has bound you since the Architect first breathed."

"And to do that," Virelith finished softly, "you must survive us."

The Gates flared with sudden light, threads tightening, shivering, humming with power. The ground trembled beneath her.

Eira swallowed, standing straighter despite the fear rising in her chest. "Then test me if that's what it takes. I am willing to do whatever I must."

The three smiled together, a sight both terrible and beautiful. "As you wish."

It was not a smile of kindness. It was hunger. The lattice screamed as it began to open. Threads writhed, coiling like serpents, snapping like whips. The ground shuddered beneath her feet.

Eira staggered, catching herself, her heart pounding. The strands whipped forward and coiled around her wrists, her waist, her throat. They burned like ice, then fire, searing through her skin. She gasped, but her voice was swallowed. The Loom had devoured her cry. Above her, the Fates leaned in.

"Peace," Solenne whispered, her smile razor thin. "Let us see if you can survive the shattering of your own thread." And the Loom closed over her.

CHAPTER 14

EIRA

The Loom did not let her fall so much as *jerk* her sideways through a slit in the world. Stone vanished, and heat fled. Eira struck something softer than marble and harder than mercy, a wooden floor where dust had gathered in tides. The air tasted of metal and old tea, of oil and charcoal. She realized where she was then. It was Adrian's apartment, and it was recognizable and so very wrong.

Paper skinned the walls in overlapping scales. Newsprint, butcher paper, canvas torn into strips. Almost every surface was smothered in lines. Not drawings in any mortal sense, but strands. Graphite had burnished them to a sickly sheen, a city of hatch marks built upon hatch marks until whole sections of wall had turned mirror black. Where there was no paper, he had used plaster. Where there was no plaster, he had used wood. The threads were every-where: crossing, tightening, pinning each other down.

Adrian crouched in the middle of the room, knees tucked to his chest, a charcoal nub gripped between thumb and forefinger. His hands were not hands anymore but instruments, their skin split, nails ragged, cuticles rimmed in black, every knuckle glossed with salve that had done nothing.

He drew on the floor because the walls were full. He drew on his shirt because the floor had no more room. He had drawn on his own wrists when his shirt was used up, creating pale lines, parallel, the ash of graphite scored into his delicate skin.

"Adrian," she breathed, the word breaking against the air, fragile and frayed.

He didn't flinch. He was listening to something she couldn't hear. Without looking up he traced a line through the open air, the nub scraping nothing, the motion so precise she could see the invisible thread he meant to follow.

"Hush," he whispered. "They're loud today. They're not in order."

Eira lowered herself as if stepping into a river whose current could take you if you move too fast. The bulb buzzed higher until it was almost a whine. Somewhere in the kitchen, the kettle had toppled but lay mercifully silent. The city outside had thinned to a dull, woolen hush, as if someone had placed felt against the windows.

She reached, very slowly, and laid two fingers against the back of his wrist. He recoiled like a struck animal. Charcoal skittered out of his grip. His head snapped toward her. The eyes she loved were bottomless now, the pupils so wide they had swallowed almost all the iris and flecks of amber clung at the edges like dying stars. For a heartbeat he didn't know her. For a heartbeat she saw her own reflection in those eyes, small, frightened, a goddess who had walked farther than she knew how to return.

"Eira?" he said at last, the word shaped cautiously.

"I'm here." She said softly, not wanting to frighten him.

"The lines are wrong," he said, holding out his trembling hands.

There were lines carved into his skin, thin at first, then deepening as though an invisible blade traced patterns only it could see.

Crimson welled in their wake, the marks burning as if lit from within. Eira pressed a hand to her mouth, stifling a gasp.

"I slept with them turned the other way and they woke up angry. If I don't put them back they sing. Hear them?" He cocked his head. "They're singing."

Adrian wasn't wrong. The room had a sound to it, under the buzz of the light bulb, under the lungs and the heartbeat and the city's woolen hush was a thin metallic hum, the note a saw makes when it kisses steel.

"Let me," Eira whispered, and folded her fingers over his. Her stillness bled outward, a tide across sand. It entered him like cool air after a fever. His breath hitched once. Twice. Slowed.

The Fates' voices drifted through the room, smooth as silk, a chorus in perfect unison.

"How tender."

"How dull."

"How will she manage without a lullaby to pour into his ear?"

The bulb flared. The hum pitched higher. On the papers near his knee, lines wriggled as if drawn by a living hand. Adrian tried to pull away and Eira didn't hold him tighter, she simply stayed.

"What if I stop," he asked, the words tumbling, "what if I stop and they fold over each other?"

Eira could hear the panic in his voice and see it etched into his face.

"There's a place where they knot, and if I sleep they pull through, I feel them pulling through my eyes, Eira!"

She put her palm against his cheek. "Breathe with me."

"When I breathe, they tangle," he said, frustration flaring through his unsteady voice. "Why did you show me? Why did you make them loud?"

"I didn't," she said, and hated the truth of it, how it meant nothing to the ache in him. "You were born with them, love. The sight was always yours."

Love. The word hung in the air like a glass ornament. She heard it break in the same instant. The room winced. The filament in the bulb screamed and settled back to its buzz like a throat hoarsened by crying.

"Always mine," he repeated, but not to her. He spoke to the walls, to the paper, and to his hands.

She took the charcoal where it lay and, without letting go of him, set the nub upright like a small, dark candle.

"Look at me," she said, and when he obeyed, her stillness folded around his shoulders like a shawl. "Even if the lines are wrong, even if they're loud, they can't drown your breath. We will count."

Adrian laughed and it was a raw, rusty sound. "What will counting do for me now?"

"We're about to find out" she said, and she began, low and steady. "In. Two. Three. Out. Two. Three."

It was not a miracle, nor magic. The hum remained, but the walls ceased their writhing, the paper no longer seemed alive, and his grip on her fingers eased, just barely. He glanced toward the nearest sheet, unaware that she was willing her essence into him, quieting his trembling form as they counted together.

"They hate this." He said, quietly.

"Then they may hate all they wish," she said, and dared a smile.

The Fates clicked their tongues, amused.

One spoke, voice bright as the underside of a knife. "*Peace as a narcotic.*"

"*Peace as bandage.*" said the second.

"*Peace as postponement,*" purred the third. "Darling, if he sleeps, the threads will only wait to gnaw at him later."

Eira ignored them. She moved her hand from his cheek to his temple, her thumb barely a weight.

"Close your eyes. Slowly." He resisted. She could feel it in the soft tremor of his jaw. Then, with a flex of will that broke her heart for its bravery, he obeyed. The first exhale shattered her. When his lashes lowered, she felt the threads graze her skin. They were not outside him, not humming in the paper or wailing in the plaster, but braided beneath his lids like filaments pulled across glass. He'd been sleeping against a loom. No wonder he woke up bleeding.

"May I?" she whispered. "If I can try to silence the threads-"

"If you take them," he interrupted, eyes still closed, voice ruthless even, "they'll have nowhere to go. They'll scream inside you."

"I have lived longer than screaming," she said, and pressed.

Eira's essence slid along the edge of his sight. It found the place where threads met nerve and then there was nothing but pain. It felt like a bright, tight ache, like knives kissing the inside of the skull. She didn't flinch. She eased her weight in, not to tear the web but to hold it. It was the most agony she had ever endured. Every inch of her, torn apart, making and remaking the fibers of her being. It was madness... it was destruction... it was... beautiful.

The impact nearly pitched her backward. It was like catching a net thrown by a storm. The lines that had scraped him with every blink now pressed their weight against her palms, her chest, even the back of her eyes. For an instant she saw what he had been seeing for days.

The city was full of bodies moving with filaments tied ankle to ankle. The old woman downstairs slept with a shimmering braid stretching from her heart to a photograph. Two boys on the corner carried a taut thread of hatred between them, one that would snap in three nights at the pitch of a single word. And above all, there was the strand that shone brighter than the rest. It was his. It curved outward, reaching, until it found her.

Her knees hit wood. She didn't remember falling. Adrian's hands were on her shoulders now, human and firm, holding her the way she had meant to hold him.

"Don't," he said fiercely. "Don't steal it. I won't let you pay for me."

"Borrow," she managed, teeth clenched. "Not

steal."

"If you keep it, they'll notice you more. They already notice you too much." His breath stuttered. "Please, Eira."

The plea in its mortal fullness was the only command that could pry her fingers from pain. She let the weight of the threads slide back to him, not into his eyes but to the edge of them, not into his skull but against her palm where they could rub against her instead of carving him raw. It was a compromise, a lie told to inevitability. The room exhaled. He opened his eyes. For the first time since she'd arrived, clarity stood there, thin and wavering but present.

Adrian lifted a hand and cupped her cheek. "Eira," he said lovingly, as if the name were the only thread he trusted. "Eira, you're hurt!"

She glanced down. Fine cuts shone along her wrists and forearms where the lines had lashed. They glowed faintly, not bleeding, full of a light that was not hers. When she flexed her fingers, the cuts tightened like embroidery pulled taut. They would scar. She suspected they were meant to.

"It's nothing," she lied.

He smiled a little. "You're terrible at lying."

"So I've been told," she said, and for a breath she felt how a home is built out of two people telling the truth where they can and forgiving where they cannot. From the ceiling, the bulb flickered off, on, off, on as if undecided whether to consent to this respite. In the kitchen, the toppled kettle released a single reluctant click.

"Sleep," she said. "I'll keep count."

"If I sleep," he whispered, "I'll dream of the scissors."

She could not promise he wouldn't. She could not promise anything. So she did what she could. She slid down the wall with him until they were seated shoulder to shoulder, her coat a poor pillow, her gown a poor blanket, the papers crackling under their combined weight.

She took his hand and began again. "In. Two. Three. Out. Two. Three."

He followed. Ten breaths. Twenty. His head tipped until it found her shoulder. The hum did not leave the room. But it lowered, like a hive in winter.

"*Peace as cradle,*" murmured one Fate, almost fondly.

"*For a moment,*" another said. "*Moments are cruel.*"

"*Show her,*" said the third, and the floor tilted.

The apartment melted to charcoal. The bulb thinned to a line of white flame and sliced itself in two. Papers sloughed from the walls like molt. Eira held Adrian's hand as the world peeled back to loom-threads and void. The Loom seized her wrist. It tried to take him with her.

"No," Eira said, and the word rang in both places.

For an instant, the Fates paid her the compliment of silence. Then the vision shifted. She was still holding his hand. But the hand had cooled. A brush lay near the fallen body. The room smelled of turpentine and honey and the heavy, irreversible quiet of a place where the living had just left.

"No," she said again, but quieter.

The word was not a bell this time. It was a prayer that knew it would not be heard. She pressed his fingers to her mouth. They were clean. No charcoal, no blood. The lines on the walls were unfinished as were her eyes, still blank on the largest canvas, as they had always been. She set his hand down carefully, as if it could break, and turned toward the door, pausing at the sight before her.

Her siblings stood in silence. Fury's jaw was set like iron, Mercy wept behind her veil, Joy's bells lay mute against her ankle, and Sorrow stretched out her hands only to let them fall, useless. Death's pale eyes lingered on her, without triumph. *This is the ending you choose,* they said in unison. *Love him, and lose him.*

Eira didn't scream. She didn't weep. She knelt and pressed her ear to his chest, knowing what she would not hear. She smoothed his hair back and kissed the place above his brow.

"If this is the price," she whispered, "take me with him."

The Fates laughed coldly, the sound like three bells tolling, three knives drawn. "*We do not barter with romance, little dove. Endings are not a market.*"

"*Choose.*" The voices hissed.

Eira closed her eyes. Inside her, something old and obedient reached for surrender. She saw the river, Thaloré's patient hands. She saw Melora's pool, Sorrow's gentleness breaking on truth. She saw the Gates and the Law, the thread and the cut, the way to make this pain stop. And then she saw him as she had first seen him, his shoulder bent to the canvas, hair falling into his eyes, his mouth soft with concentration. Imperfect and beautiful. Mortal. Not a prophet, not a sacrifice, not a puppet. Adrian.

"I refuse," she said, and her voice belonged to the piece of her that had learned, finally, the difference between holding and clinging. "I will not choose your futures. I will make one."

Something tore, not in her, but in the fabric that held the room. The corpse-smell fled. The brush leapt back to the table. His hand warmed under hers. The apartment folded itself right-side-out with an audible shudder. The hum returned, spiteful and small. She opened her eyes to find him breathing. It was shallow and he seemed exhausted, but he was alive. Alive.

Adrian was alive.

Eira let out a breath she would measure the rest of her days against.

"*Stubborn,*" crooned a Fate.

"*Expensive,*" said another.

"*Next,*" purred the third, and the floor gave way again.

As the Loom yanked her onward, Eira held to the heat of his palm as long as the law of the place allowed. The last sensation to leave her was the weight of his fingers tightening once, on purpose, as if he'd reached up through the tremor and chosen her back. Then the walls became lines. The lines became knives. The knives became light. And the next horror was unleashed.

CHAPTER 15

EIRA

Eira felt as if the Loom had devoured her, snatching her away from the one thing she tried to tether herself to. The threads violently seized her limbs, her throat, her heart, winding themselves through her veins until she felt less body than fabric. They burned cold, then hot, alternating until pain blurred into something worse, the sensation of being rewritten. Each heartbeat no longer felt like her own. Each thought trembled, unsure whether it belonged to her or to the thing that now held her.

Eira gasped, but no sound passed her lips. Her cry was caught, smothered. The Loom had swallowed her voice. The light around her split into a thousand strands, infinite colors vibrating with hunger. They wove across her vision, some glimmering with warmth, others black and jagged, cutting even the light itself. For a moment she thought she could see them all, every thread of every soul, weaving past her into eternity. Then the sight was yanked away, and she was thrown forward.

She landed hard on her knees. Stone met her palms and felt cool, polished, impossibly smooth. She staggered to her feet and looked around. She was standing in a great hall, but it was no place she had ever known. The ceiling soared high into shadow, a dome painted with images that shifted and writhed, stars burning, wars breaking, oceans rising.

Fires flickered and were snuffed out. Children cried and grew silent. Empires rose and crumbled. All of it moved across the stone as though it were alive. At the far end of the hall, a figure stood on a dais. Adrian.

Her breath caught. His dark hair fell loose about his shoulders, glinting in the firelight. His robes were white and gold, rich as any king's, embroidered with patterns that shifted like threads in motion. His skin shone with a faint radiance, as though lit from within. When he lifted his head, his eyes glowed amber, catching the light and holding it.

"Eira," he said, his voice echoing through the vast chamber. "You came."

She stumbled forward. "Adrian?"

He raised a hand. The hall hushed, and the fires stilled. The silence was total, a silence not of peace but of command.

"My love," Adrian said, and his voice reverberated like prophecy. "Look what you have made of me."

Her chest tightened. "Made?"

He stepped down from the dais, each footfall ringing like a bell. When he reached her, he took her hands in his. His grip was warm, strong. He leaned close, his eyes brilliant, almost too bright.

"You gave me sight," he whispered. "You showed me the threads. With you, I see everything. The weave of kings and beggars, of storms and empires. They bow before me because I speak their fate aloud."

As if summoned, the hall filled with people. Shadows of mortals streamed in from every side, faces turned upward toward him. They knelt, hands clasped, mouths moving in prayer. Their whispers rose and fell in waves, all chanting *"Adrian!" "Adrian!" "Adrian!"*

Eira's heart pounded as she surveyed her surroundings. "This… this is not real."

He smiled, radiant, too radiant. "Is it not? They hear me, Eira. They need me. And I need you."

He lifted her hands, kissing her knuckles reverently. "Stay by me, and the world will never know chaos again."

For a single, terrible moment, she almost believed him. The sight of him like this, regal, adored, powerful beyond measure, filled her with fierce pride. She thought of all the centuries she had carried the burden of stillness, unseen, unheard. And here was Adrian, mortal and fragile, wielding the weight of prophecy. Her Adrian. But then her gaze slipped. She took notice of the people kneeling before him. It was their eyes. They didn't look how eyes should look… they were hollow. Vacant. Devoid of everything.

They whispered his name, but their voices were flat, lifeless, like wind through reeds. Their faces did not smile, did not weep. They only repeated.

"Adrian," she whispered, her throat tight.

He smiled still, but his teeth gleamed too sharp, his glow too fierce. "Yes. Speak it. Speak me into eternity, my love!"

She tore her hands from his. "This is not you."

The glow flickered. For a heartbeat his eyes went wide, his face contorted, as though something beneath the radiance clawed to escape. Then he straightened, the smile fixed again. The crowd whispered louder, the sound now a hiss. *Adrian! Adrian! Adrian!*

Eira stepped back, shaking her head. "No. You are kind. You are gentle. You are not this."

The vision trembled. The painted dome above cracked, spilling threads of light. The crowd hissed, their eyes hollow. Adrian's form shimmered, tearing at the edges like cloth too tightly stretched.

Then the voices of the Fates poured through the hall, layered and amused.

"Would you not prefer this?"

"*Beloved of thousands.*"

"*Crowned in light.*"

Eira pressed her hands over her ears, but the voices were inside her head, vibrating through her bones. "This is not him!" she cried.

The hall shattered. The threads yanked her again, dragging her screaming into another vision.

CHAPTER 16
EIRA

Threads wrapped her waist and throat, pulling, dragging her toward another vision. The air around her thrummed with inevitability, the song of scissors sharpening. She tried to fight it, but resisted using her Sovereign nature against the Fates. She resisted the urge to start a war she wasn't sure she could win on her own. Then everything broke.

Light snapped. The strands shivered, recoiling as though struck. The Loom screamed, its voice not sound but the tearing of every thread at once. Eira fell hard onto stone that should not have been there, onto a floor slick with shadow and rain. She lay gasping, her chest heaving, her skin still burning from where the threads had scored her. For a moment she thought it was another illusion. Another torment. But then she heard them, the familiar voices, heavy with power, weight, and memory.

She raised her head and her heart faltered. They were there. Every one of them. The Sovereigns. Fury stood at the front, hair snapping in a wind without source, eyes molten fire. Mercy shifted beside him, her silver veil trembling as faint light poured from her hands. Rain fell only around Sorrow, soaking her indigo gown, streaking her pale, solemn face. At the end of the line, Death towered, motionless, his crown of bones glinting cold against the dark.

Pain stepped forward in crimson silk that cut the air like knives. Pleasure followed, beauty sharpened to danger, her smile edged and hollow. Revenge lingered, smirk sharp as steel, his presence slicing the space around him. Joy was silent, her bells stilled, a single nod her only sound. And Life shone radiant and luminous, a golden sword blazing in her hands.

All nine of her siblings had stepped into the Loom. They had come for her. Eira staggered to her knees. Her auburn hair clung damp to her cheeks, her gown in tatters.

"No," she whispered, her throat raw. "You shouldn't be here."

"You shouldn't either," Thaloré said. Death's voice rolled like a bell struck deep underwater. Shadows curled at his feet, coiling, restless.

Fury's voice cracked through the air, loud as thunder. "They mean to break you, Peace, but they will not! You are a Sovereign, and we do not break easily."

"They will break all of us for this," Sorrow murmured. Her rain fell harder, dripping into the cracks of the marble floor, steaming where it touched Fury's flames. "You know the punishment."

"They already punish us," Mercy said, her voice thin, trembling behind her veil. "The Balance howls. The rifts grow wider every day. You all feel it."

The Loom groaned. Threads rippled outward, vibrating in fury, the Gates behind them flaring with violent light. The air smelled of smoke and ozone, of endings. A hiss rose through the chamber, echoing a thousand voices woven into one. The Fates' laughter followed, silken and terrible.

"Oh, how bold."

"How reckless."

"How delicious."

Threads lashed down like whips. Fury roared, his arms blazing, fire tearing the strands apart before they could strike. Death lifted a single hand, and shadows swallowed the threads whole, binding them midair. Sorrow spread her arms, and her rain hardened to a veil of water that hissed as it met the light. Revenge stepped forward, his hands sheathed in steel that was not steel, slicing through what dared come near him.

Eira rose to her feet, every part of her trembling. Her siblings were not supposed to be here. The Law forbade it. To enter the Loom was to risk being cut from existence. And yet, here they stood, together.

"Why?" Her voice broke on the word. "Why risk everything for me? This will end you all. This will end everything!"

Revenge turned his sharp gaze on her, his smile thin. "Because, little sister, just like Balance, choice should also be sacred. Not a death sentence."

Pleasure laughed, a sound like velvet tearing. "And because, little dove, we are so very tired of chains."

Zivael lifted her radiant hands, and light flared from her palms, burning threads to ash. Yet her ethereal face was grim, eyes hollow with knowledge. "You have stirred something none of us dared to admit. We are bound, Eira, as you are bound. To step here is to admit it."

The Loom screamed again. The walls of light shook, threads quivering, tightening, furious. The Fates' voices split the air, no longer amused.

"They dare."

"They challenge us!"

"They will be unmade."

More threads lashed downward, sharper than lightning, faster than flame. Fury's fire faltered. Mercy cried out, raising her hands, light spilling but too thin to shield them all. Pain hissed and struck back with blades of scarlet silk. Death's shadows swelled, but even they trembled.

The Loom was trying to cut them out. Eira's heart pounded. The threads still coiled in her own flesh, glowing wounds searing across her arms and chest. Her siblings fought around her, but she knew the Loom's fury would only grow.

In that chaos she realized the Sovereigns had not come only to save her. They had come to break the Law itself, and reshape their destinies.

THE MARBLE SHOOK beneath their feet, fissures splitting outward like cracks in ice. Threads hissed through the air, snapping down in whips of color. Fury bellowed, striking fire against them, burning them to cinders. Death raised a wall of shadow, the strands hissing as they tried to cut through. Still, they came.

Eira stood in the eye of it, trembling, her body a map of glowing wounds. Every thread that lashed the air felt as though it lashed her skin again.

"This is madness," Sorrow cried, her rain hardening to a curtain of water that steamed when touched by light.

She turned on Fury, her pale eyes fierce despite her grief. "Do you know what they'll do now that we're here?"

"What they always do," Fury spat, his fire flaring, his jaw locked. "Bind us. Chain us. Clip our wings and call it Balance."

"They'll cut us out entirely!" Mercy wailed, her silver veil trembling as she pressed her glowing hands outward, warding a cluster of threads from striking Eira. "I feel the scissors already, don't you? They wait above us, waiting to fall!"

"They wait above her," Pain said coldly, her crimson gown trailing as she stepped lightly through the chaos, her knives singing as she severed strands. "And if they fall on her, they fall on all of us. We are bound more tightly than we admit."

"Then why save her?" Joy demanded suddenly. She stood near the edge of the circle, her bells silenced, her eyes shadowed with something that looked uncomfortably like envy.

"Why not let Peace fall? Perhaps the world would be stronger without her." Eira flinched as though struck.

Fury turned on Joy, his fire snapping. "Because she is ours."

"Because she is yours," Joy shot back, bitterness sharp in her tone. "Do not speak for me."

"Enough." Death's voice cut through them all like a tolling bell. Shadows deepened as he stepped forward, his pale eyes fixing on Eira. "We are not here to squabble. We are here because Peace has done what none of us dared to do! She challenged the Law, and none of us were bold enough to do so, even though we are the Sovereigns. We are eternal, and we alone govern the Pantheon. Yet we are bound by rules governed by the Fates!"

Revenge's smile was thin, his gaze like sharpened steel. "So true, brother. And in breaking the Law, Peace has proved the Law is not unbreakable.

That is why I am here." His eyes glinted as he parried a flash of light with a blade conjured from his palm. "To see it undone."

"You would burn the whole of Balance just for vengeance," Sorrow murmured, her voice a weight of mourning.

"Better vengeance than obedience," Revenge snarled.

Pleasure laughed, low and velvet, her perfume cutting oddly through the air of smoke and rain. "And better desire than chains. Tell me you haven't dreamed of it, dear Sorrow. Tell me you haven't longed for something the Law denied you."

Sorrow's rain faltered for a moment, her head bowing, her lips pressed tight. Eira staggered, staring at them all. The floor trembled under her, the Loom roaring louder, its fury rising like a storm. Threads lashed, and still her siblings argued, their voices cutting over one another, centuries of bitterness breaking loose in the heat of defiance.

"Stop!" she cried, her voice almost hoarse. They all turned to her. Her chest heaved, her hands trembling, the glowing wounds on her arms searing bright. "You shouldn't be here. Not for me. Not for this. If they cut you out, if they unmake you-"

"They won't," Fury said, his fire flaring higher. "Not while we stand together."

"That is the problem," Death said, his tone flat. His pale eyes shifted to the threads quivering above them. "Together, we are too dangerous. They will not suffer it long."

The Loom groaned, its threads tightening, the Gates behind them pulsing with violent light. The hiss grew louder, the word Trespass woven into the air. The Fates' laughter cut through again, sharper this time.

"Oh, how fragile."

"Oh, how foolish."

"Oh, how close."

It was then Eira realized that her siblings were not united. They had come for her, yes, but for themselves too. For vengeance. For freedom. For desire. For their own grief. And if the Loom forced them to choose, to save her, or to save themselves, she did not know which way they would turn.

CHAPTER 17
EIRA

The Loom screamed. Threads lashed down like a storm of blades, faster, sharper, heavier. Fury's fire guttered. Sorrow's rain hissed into steam. Mercy collapsed under the weight of the light. Even Death staggered, his shadows sliced thin as paper. They could not hold much longer.

Eira bent double, every strike searing her flesh anew. Her body was a map of glowing wounds, each cut pulling tighter, threatening to unravel her. She tasted iron in her mouth. She could feel the scissors above, ready to fall. This is how it ends, she thought. Not with choice. Not with love. With silence. Then Fury roared, voice shaking the chamber. "No more chains!" His fire flared wild, licking at the very walls of the Loom.

Revenge's blades sang, slashing upward. Sorrow spread her arms, rain falling so hard it was thunder. One by one the Sovereigns cried out, their voices overlapping in defiance.

"Sovereigns will not be bound!"

"We won't be shackled any longer!"

"We won't be silenced by any Law!"

Their voices carried beyond the Loom. Beyond the threads.

Beyond even the Fates. And something heard. The air split, the marble beneath their feet cracking like an eggshell. Between the shards of light, between the screams of the Loom, a deeper sound rumbled. Not laughter. Not fury. The sound of galaxies turning, of suns igniting, of black holes breathing. The Cosmos had woken.

Eira gasped, falling to her knees. She knew it instantly. The force older than them all, their mother and father both. The Architect and the Void. The First Breath and the Last Silence.

The threads recoiled, hissing. The Gates bent inward, folding like cloth. The Fates' voices split the air, sharper than razors, in unison:

"They dare-"

"They call-"

"They will be-"

But their words faltered, for The Cosmos spoke. Not with a voice, but with a tremor in every bone. *"Enough."*

The Loom shook. The threads writhed, twitching as if in agony. And then the Sovereigns were torn from it, carried on a tide of starlight and shadow. Eira clutched her chest as the world spun, her siblings' voices fading into nothing, until she struck soft ground, the grass beneath her as smooth as velvet.

There was silence until Eira opened her eyes, realizing she was back in her realm. The still waters lay before her, glassy and endless, reflecting dawn that never shifted. The air smelled of soft rain and early wind. Her throne stood in the distance, untouched. She was home.

Her siblings staggered around her, gasping, their forms flickering with exhaustion. Fury collapsed to one knee, his flames dim. Mercy pressed her hands together, trembling. Even Death's shadows flickered faintly at his feet. They had escaped, by their parents' hand. Eira rose unsteadily, clutching her arms, her chest still burning.

Eira turned, her voice breaking. "Adrian?" Silence answered, and her heart lurched. "No." Her voice came out in a weak whisper.

Her siblings looked up, their eyes grim. Eira stumbled forward, using her essence to search the mortal realm for him. Her chest tore open with panic.

"Where is he? WHERE IS HE?" she screamed, almost hysterical.

Sorrow stepped close, her rain falling soft against Eira's arm. Her voice was quiet. "The Loom took him, sister."

Eira closed her eyes, her essence echoing the truth of her sister's words.

Her still realm rippled, the glassy water trembling, shivering as though mirroring the ache in her chest. For the first time in eternity, Peace's domain shook with unrest.

Eira fell to her knees, her voice raw. "No... No, no, no!"

A guttural cry tore from her throat and she didn't realize it was her own until she felt arms wrap around her. The siblings stood behind her, silent, as Sorrow comforted her. Their faces were grim and shadowed. Even Fury had no fire, her sister Mercy at a loss for words.

Adrian was gone. And the Loom had him. The waters of Eira's realm no longer lay still. They quivered in uneasy ripples, reflecting her panic back at her a thousandfold. The sky, usually serene dawn light, roiled faintly with pale storm clouds. The seat of Peace herself trembled as though it feared her sorrow.

Adrian should have been there with her. But he was gone. Her siblings gathered in a fractured circle behind her, every face dim with exhaustion and something sharper. Fear. Anger. Unease.

Fury paced, flames sparking at his heels, his jaw tight enough to crack stone. "The Loom has him. That's the end. Mortals don't return once it takes them."

"Then we go back," Eira said, her voice sharp, trembling. "We tear it open, we drag him free, and we END them! We are Sovereigns. WE were there in the beginning, and we can begin their end."

"You'd damn us all!" Joy snapped, her bells clattering faintly as she threw her hands wide. "We barely survived once. Do you want to see what the scissors will do if we step foot there again?"

Eira whirled on her. "Do you think I care what they do to me?" Her voice cracked across the realm like thunder. The still waters trembled harder.

Mercy lifted her silver-veiled face, tears glistening beneath the gauze. "Peace...you cannot."

"I must!" Eira cried, her chest heaving. "You saw what they did. He is mine. He is MINE. I have never had anyone, anything to myself! I have played my role well for eons, but Adrian is mine. They cannot have him."

"He is more than yours, sister." The voice was calm, deep, and terrible. Thaloré spoke, not as her brother, but as Death. The others stilled. Eira froze, her auburn hair falling wild across her shoulders, golden eyes blazing.

"What do you mean?" she asked, her words edged with both confusion and anger.

Death stepped forward, his pale crown casting shadows that swallowed the light. His gaze fixed on her, grave and certain. "Did you never wonder why he saw the threads? Why he could paint what should not be painted, dream what no mortal should?"

"I knew he was a Seer," she said, her voice breaking. "The Watcher told me as much, but I-"

"Not only a Seer." Thaloré's words dropped like stones into the water as he cut her off, as a parent would comforting a small child. "He is a descendant. The last remnant of a line long thought severed. His blood carries the gift of the old gods."

Eira staggered back, her breath catching. "What gods?"

"The ones before us," Sorrow whispered, stepping forward, her rain falling soft around her. Her indigo gown clung heavy with grief, her face pale. "The Greeks. The Pantheon the mortals worshiped before the Architect sealed their lineages. Their power was meant to fade. But it did not. It slept." She lifted her gaze, heavy with knowledge. "And Adrian is proof it still breathes."

Eira's throat closed. "Which god? Tell me, which one?"

Sorrow's lips trembled. "Apollo." The name carried weight, echoing throughout the stillness like a chord struck on a harp. "God of light. Of prophecy. Of art."

Death's pale eyes narrowed as he spoke. "His blood made Adrian more than mortal. It gave him the gift to see what others cannot. The Loom did not take him by chance. It took him because he belongs to it."

"No," Eira whispered. Her knees buckled, and she sank to the floor. "No, he is not theirs. He is mine. He is…"

Realization and horror washed over her as her voice went cold. "He is our enemy… He is our undoing…" Her voice broke, tears spilling hot and unrestrained down her cheeks. "But still, he is mine."

Fury's fire crackled hotter, anger rolling off him in waves. "If Apollo's blood flows in him, then he is dangerous. Perhaps more dangerous than even you, sister."

"Dangerous?" Eira snapped, lifting her tear- streaked face to him. "Or precious? Do you think the Loom would risk itself? No. There is more to this!"

Sorrow moved closer, kneeling by her side, her rain mingling with Eira's tears. Her voice was soft, a lullaby heavy with grief. "Maybe he completes them. Together, the Fates and the Loom can destroy us." The realm shook at the words. The siblings shifted uneasily.

Eira closed her eyes, her voice raw. "Then we will take him back. Even if the Fates themselves must bleed. I will tear Fate itself apart if it means he breathes beside me again."

The silence after Eira's vow stretched taut. Her words echoed in the still waters of her realm until they were almost a song.

At last, Death spoke. His voice was steady, carved from stone and shadow. "There is more you must know."

Eira turned, her eyes blazing, throat raw. "No one thought to tell me this when you discovered it?" Her voice cut through the silence like a blade, but Death's gaze did not falter.

"I'm surprised the Threads did not reveal it to you as they did to us in the Loom. They showed us the truth."

Eira looked around at her siblings, confusion etched across her face. "What else is there? What else do I not know?"

Death continued, unfazed by her anger, "You think him a distant descendant, blood diluted by centuries of mortal lives. That would be dangerous enough. But it is not the truth. Adrian Lysander is not only of Apollo's line. He is a demigod."

The word rippled through the chamber like a wave striking shore. Joy gasped, her bells clattering faintly. Mercy staggered, clutching her veil. Fury snarled, fire snapping. Even Sorrow bowed her head as though in mourning. Eira froze, her blood running cold.

"A... demigod?" Eira whispered, disbelief and awe rippling through her chest.

"Yes." Death's eyes did not waver. "His blood is not diluted beyond meaning. It burns. His father was mortal, yes, but his mother...was not."

The world tilted beneath her.

"Do you mean to say..." Eira started but was interrupted.

"His mother was a goddess," Sorrow whispered, her voice fragile but steady. "A forgotten daughter of Apollo's house, hidden when the old Pantheon fell. She bore him in silence, raised him in shadows, then vanished into dust when her thread was cut. Adrian grew believing himself mortal. But he is not. He is half of two worlds. Mortal flesh, immortal blood."

Eira pressed her hand to her lips, her body trembling. Images of him flooded her all at once. Adrian smiling with his brush steady in hand, his laughter rare and precious, the strange light in his eyes when he spoke of dreams. It all fit now. His sight of the threads. His gift for creation. The way the Loom had looked at him, hungry and waiting.

Pleasure stepped forward, her perfume thick and cloying, her smile too wide. "A demigod. Do you know what that means, sister? He was never yours alone. The Loom will shape him into its mouthpiece. A vessel. And oh, what a vessel he will make, with blood like that."

Fury's voice cracked the air, low and dangerous. "Or a weapon."

Mercy cried out, wringing her hands. "No! Don't say it like that! No good can come from that at all. What a sad fate for our dear sister."

"Adrian?" Revenge scoffed, his eyes sharp. "Call him what he is. He is a godling. A demigod. That is why the Loom took him. That is why Balance strains around us even now. They don't steal for amusement. They steal what matters."

"He matters because he is mine!" Eira's voice broke through them all, fierce and trembling. Her realm quaked, waters rippling violently. "Not for what his blood gives him. Not for prophecy or power. For who he is! The man who saw my nature without fear. The man who laughed when no one else could make me laugh."

Her fists clenched, her wounds blazing silver- gold. "Do not strip him down to bloodlines and destiny. He is more than that."

Sorrow stepped closer, her rain mingling with Eira's tears. "But the Loom does not see him as you do. To them, he is not Adrian. He is Apollo's echo. The last seed of a forgotten Pantheon. And that makes him priceless."

Eira's heart clenched so hard she thought it might tear. Sorrow's glow dimmed as she spoke, her voice heavy with truth.

"Peace...there have been no demigods since the Architect set the Laws in motion with the Fates. That bloodline should have ended. Yet somehow it did not. Do you not see? Adrian is a violation of the old order. His existence alone is a rebellion."

The siblings exchanged glances. Fury's flames guttered low, Mercy's silver veil quivered, Sorrow's rain fell heavier, and Revenge's blade-like smile gleamed faint.

Eira, trembling in her anger, whispered the truth aloud. "He is mine. MINE. And I will not let the Loom keep him, nor the Architect destroy him."

The still waters rippled again, shivering like glass. On the surface, faint and terrible, she thought she saw Adrian's reflection. His dark hair falling into his eyes, his brush steady in his hand. And then, just as swiftly, it was gone.

CHAPTER 18
ADRIAN

Darkness. Not the absence of light, but the pressure of it. Adrian felt it pressing into his chest, threading through his veins, crawling behind his eyes. The Loom had taken him, torn him from the safety of her realm, from the warmth of her hand. Now it filled him, humming, whispering, pulling at the pieces of him it already owned. He sat on a cold floor, though he could not see it.

His wrists were bound, not with rope, but with living strands that shifted and bit when he moved. His throat burned as if a voice not his own strained to speak through him. And still, he smiled faintly. Because none of this was new.

The Loom's voice shivered in his bones.

"Show us."

"Show us what you are."

He closed his eyes and let it wash over him. He had resisted for years, scribbling the threads in charcoal and paint, pretending they were visions he could not explain. He had built his life around the silence, around the lie that he was only a man. But he wasn't. He never had been.

The memory returned, sharp as a blade.

ADRIAN WAS EIGHT YEARS OLD, *sitting by a window cracked open to the spring air. His mother's hand lay over his, her skin fever-hot, her breath uneven. The light caught her hair in a way that never seemed entirely human, and for the first time he noticed how her eyes were too bright, like sunlight poured into glass.*

She had pressed her lips to his brow and whispered, "You are not like the others, Adrian. You are my son, but also his. The god of light, of prophecy, of song. Apollo's blood runs in you."

His child's heart had stuttered. "A god?"

Her smile trembled, fierce and sorrowful. "A demigod. The last. They will not understand. If they know, they will come for you. The Loom will never let you go."

She had coughed then, the sound tearing her small body, but she gripped his shoulders hard enough to bruise. "Promise me. Never show them. Not the visions. Not the glow. Hide it, and bury false memories in your mind until you cannot any longer."

"I promise," he had whispered, crying into her lap.

She had kissed his hair, her tears falling into it. "Good boy. My bright boy. Hide the light. One day, it will burn too strong to contain. But not yet. Not yet."

THE MEMORY FADED, leaving only the present. His mother's words had lived in him like iron shackles. And for years, he had kept them. Even from Eira. Especially from her. But the Loom knew. The strands writhed tighter around him, searing his skin, hissing for revelation. *Show us! Show us!*

Adrian exhaled slowly. And this time, he did not resist. Light bled from his skin. Faint at first, then brighter, until the chamber glowed with it. His hair lifted in the current of it, gold threaded into the black. His eyes opened, no longer midnight but molten amber, burning from within. The threads that bound him recoiled, and the light raced through them, singing, bending them to his pulse.

The Loom shivered. Adrian rose to his feet, taller than he had ever felt, his chest alive with a heat that was not fire but something older, something purer. He raised his hands, and the strands bent toward them, forced still. A demigod. Apollo's son. The last of a silenced line. He had known it all along.

The smile that curved his lips was not cruel, but certain. "You wanted me," he murmured into the Loom's trembling silence. "Now you have me. But you will never own me."

The chamber quaked, and the Loom screamed. And in the echo of that sound, Adrian understood the truth that chilled him even as the light poured from his veins. This was only the beginning.

EPILOGUE

The world slept. It was not night. It was not death, but silence. One by one, cities dimmed, villages hushed, fields grew still. Infants ceased their cries, birds folded their wings, waves forgot how to break. Even the wind seemed to bow its head. A silent sleep fell across the mortal world, heavy and absolute. And above it, in the infinite dark, the Sovereigns walked.

Together, the siblings ventured where few had dared, into the heart of the Cosmos, to the Chasm. Their birth parent. Their source. The Architect and The Void, the First Breath and the Last Silence.

It stirred as they approached, the air trembling with the weight of suns being born and extinguished. The Chasm inhaled, and stars flared. It exhaled, and galaxies trembled. Then, with a sigh that spanned eternity, it began to take form. Light folded into shape. Darkness draped itself into curves. In moments, a body stood before them, beautiful, incomprehensible, a living reflection of every mortal dream of divinity.

The Chasm had manifested in a corporeal form, and when it opened its eyes, the siblings felt as though they were children again.

"*My children,*" it said, its voice the chorus of every element, fire and rain and stone and wind. "*You have torn at the Loom. You have woken what should have slept. And you have seen what was always coming.*"

The Sovereigns bowed their heads, though unease writhed among them.

Eira's chest burned as she stepped forward. "Adrian..." Her voice trembled. "The Loom has him. He-"

"*I know, my child.*" Chasm said gently. "*Your brother knew as well. He knew this was coming.*"

The siblings stiffened. Fury's fire guttered. Mercy's veil quivered. Joy's bells shivered against her ankle. They exchanged looks. Confusion. Suspicion.

"What brother?" Sorrow whispered, her rain falling soft in the endless dark.

The Chasm only smiled, eyes alight with galaxies.

And then a voice answered from behind them. "You have forgotten me. But I have not forgotten you."

They turned as the figure stepped from the starlight, tall and slender, robed in cloth the color of inked parchment and constellations. His hair fell black as obsidian, streaked faintly with silver, his eyes vast and sharp, as though they contained the whole of thought itself.

Caelus.

Knowledge.

Their brother. Long forgotten. Long erased. Yet standing now before them, calm as if he had never left.

Eira staggered back, her heart lurching. "Where have you been all this time?" her voice trailed off, as she tried to make sense of the events unfolding.

Fury's flames flickered uncertainly, Pain lowered her blades, and even Death bowed his head. Some memory stirred in them, faint and aching, as if their minds had been forced to forget what their souls had always known.

Caelus looked at them each in turn, his expression neither cold nor warm, only knowing. "Something has been unleashed," he said softly, the weight of his words pressing into their bones. "Something that was never meant to walk this earth."

His gaze lingered on Eira last, and the silver in his eyes glowed brighter. "And now, sister... the choice is no longer yours alone to make."

BONUS CHAPTERS

BONUS CHAPTER ONE: EIRA

Nothing about Eira's realm felt peaceful anymore. She could find no joy, no hope now that Adrian was with *them*, suffering at *their* hands. Or perhaps *they* suffered at *his*. She did not know, and she had not dared reach out to find him with her essence.

She stood barefoot at the edge of the water, hair loose around her shoulders, gown brushing softly against her skin. Eira's realm echoed her unrest, shifting to reflect her mood. The air thrummed softly, as if answering the beat of her heart.

She pressed her palm over her chest as she closed her eyes, thinking of *him*. The ache there had not dulled, and she did not think it ever would. It burned as fiercely as the day he was torn from her.

Adrian.

His name was both balm and blade, a solace to her chaos. She could still see his face when she closed her eyes. She pictured the curve of his smile, and his eyes that reminded her of dark pools of midnight. She couldn't help but conjure an image in her mind of the way he had looked at her as if she were the sum of all beginnings and endings. She had loved him in that small, impossible space where love and disobedience met, and now she bore the consequences.

But Adrian had lied. He lied about who he was, hid the truth of his blood behind those midnight eyes that held too much curiosity, too much love, too much *everything* to be contained in one man. That truth still bled, no matter how hard she tried to soften it with reason.

Eira turned from the water, anger flashing sharp beneath her grief. "You should have told me," she whispered into the wind. "You should have trusted me."

Her realm shuddered at her tone as a faint hum reverberated through the water. Eira knew it was a warning from Balance itself. Peace was not meant to feel wrath, for she was Peace. That was her nature, her duty. And in her disruption of balance, she had corrupted her very nature. Her anger threatened the very laws she embodied, but she could not stop feeling. She could not stop longing, wishing Adrian were here with her.

"He knew," she hissed to no one who could hear. "He knew what he was. He looked at me with mortal eyes while hiding the blood of a god. How dare he!"

"Would it have changed the outcome had he told you?" A voice came softly, carried on the still air.

Eira spun, eyes blazing with a mixture of fury and caution.

A tall figure stood where the horizon met the lake, robed in twilight, constellations sewn into the fabric of his mantle. His dark hair fell in loose obsidian waves to his shoulders, faint silver streaks glinting. His eyes held galaxies, and the vast knowledge of existence. Caelus—the forgotten brother, Sovereign of Knowledge.

A shiver ran through her as she stared at him, unease curling low in her stomach. "I remember you," Eira said slowly, stepping toward him. "But ... I do not. You were gone, and now you are here, and I do not know how I ever forgot you. How did I forget you, brother?"

Caelus tilted his head slightly, his expression unreadable. "Because you were made to forget, Eira."

Her pulse quickened and her brows scrunched as she stared into his eyes, looking for a hidden truth that was not yet revealed. "By whom?"

"The time is not right for you to hold that knowledge," Caelus said, his voice quiet but certain. "But I can tell you ... things have changed and the truth will be revealed soon."

Eira's throat tightened. "I am sure this must be dire if you have come back."

His lips curved faintly, not quite a smile. "Sister, it was always going to happen this way. No matter which path you chose."

He stepped closer, the constellations on his robe glinting faintly with each movement. "You once came to me for counsel, long ago. You asked if love could exist without consequence for us. I told you no, but you have always been curious. You are not the first."

Eira looked away, ashamed and defiant all at once. "Then tell me now, Caelus. What consequence comes of loving a demigod bound by The Fates? I cannot have him, and I do not know how to save him without starting a war."

She looked away, her eyes shining with silver tears. She couldn't banish the hurt, couldn't reconcile it with the love she still felt for him.

"I did not know," she said softly, setting her jaw. "I did not know what he truly was. I am so angry, brother."

Caelus' gaze softened. "You are not angry because of his omission, Eira. You are angry because he loved you enough to protect you from the truth."

Her breath hitched, a soft gasp escaping as the truth of his words pierced the place where love still lingered. Caelus stepped closer, his presence strangely comforting.

"He hid what he was so you would not bear the weight of what that meant. His blood is prophecy, and his heart is light. Adrian could be considered a weapon because his blood has ties to the old gods, but I do not believe he was ever a weapon forged against you."

Eira met his eyes, her fury dissolving into confusion. "How can I get him back? How can I release him from The Three Fates?"

Caelus looked out over the water, his expression distant. "That is best discussed another time. And right now, I do not have much of it."

The water rippled violently, light flashing beneath its surface as Eira took a step back, her gown sweeping around her legs. "Can Adrian be freed? Could I go to him now?"

"Perhaps," Caelus said, his voice barely a whisper. "But if you try, you may very well destroy Balance in the process."

"I would destroy everything that keeps him from me," Eira said sharply, clenching her fists as she lifted her face to the sky. The golden threads shimmered overhead, glinting as though answering her defiance.

Caelus smiled, not a true smile, but a sorrowful curve of his lips. "You sound like you mean that."

"I don't think I've ever spoken truer words," she said, her voice low but firm.

They stood in silence for a long moment, watching the light tremble on the water. Then Eira asked, softer, "Why did I forget you, Caelus? Truly?"

He turned to her, his eyes vast and knowing. "Because when I left, I took the memory with me. That is all I can say."

"What did you know?" she whispered.

"I know all things. But would it change anything if you knew?" he said gently. "Sometimes it is best to let things unfold the way they were intended."

Eira felt something inside her fracture. This uncertainty was foreign to her and she was out of patience, tired of waiting.

"Tell me what I have to become to save him," she murmured, looking off. "I cannot be Peace when my heart is in ruin. Who must I become, Caelus?"

Caelus' voice lowered as he looked to the sky, then back at her.

"Something more than Peace. More than what your nature allows you to be."

When Eira looked back, he was gone. Only fragments of starlight remained, dissolving into the air. She stood alone, her reflection rippling in the lake. The horizon quivered faintly, as if the world itself knew what was to come.

"If I must become something more," she whispered, "then heavens help the ones who caused it."

BONUS CHAPTER TWO: ADRIAN

The Loom shuddered as Adrian explored its endless expanse. Every thread within sight rippled outward, creating an ocean of light and shadow folding over itself. Adrian stood unmoving at its center, radiating golden light.

"So what will you show me now that you know you can't keep me?" His voice was low but carried throughout the expanse. "Show me the cost. Let me see the world you guard so desperately."

The threads flared to life instantly, obeying his command. The Loom answered to no one, yet it wanted Adrian to see. It was eager to show him what was to come.

Scenes poured through the threads, flashing across Adrian's mind. There were millions of lives stitched into the same endless fabric, each following their own thread. He saw what had been, and what was yet to come—and he watched, unmoving.

The tapestry pulsed with heartbeat after heartbeat until it was almost too much to bear. But Adrian endured. He *would* endure, for he was no mere mortal. He was born of the blood of gods.

"This is what you will break if you stay on your path," The Loom whispered. Its voice rumbled like thunder pressed through glass. It

was impossible to locate, woven through every thread, seeping into his thoughts.

"*Every breath, every name, every moment. You risk destroying Balance.*"

Golden light burned in Adrian's eyes as they hardened with resolve. "Maybe the world would be better off without your leash."

"*Without design there is nothing. Chaos does not nurture, child of light. It devours. And we will not allow that.*"

Adrian's jaw set, anger simmering just beneath the surface. "You will not hold me, and I WILL get back to Eira."

"*She is being undone by you. By your very existence,*" The Loom whispered.

"She will be *freed* by me," he said, closing his eyes against the storm of light.

The Loom's vibration deepened until the light around him became a wrathful storm. Threads lashed through the air like whips striking toward him, but Adrian would not yield. He lifted his arm and the blows scattered against a flare of golden light that burst from his skin.

"I will not bow," he said. "Not to you. Not to your Architect."

"*Balance is order. Order is survival,*" The Loom hissed.

"Then maybe survival isn't enough," Adrian shot back, defiantly.

The air cracked and the web of threads drew itself tight, pulling in until every strand converged on him, binding him in living light. His limbs locked and his breath left him in a gasp. But Adrian was resilient; he had to be. The blood of Apollo ran in his veins, and he would not be silenced as the old gods were.

"*You are not the first to defy Balance,*" The Loom's voice vibrated throughout him. "*The old gods were banished for it. The Architect bound them to keep the world from dissolving. Surely you know this, child of light. When you tamper with Balance there is always a price.*"

"And yet, here I am," Adrian rasped, struggling against the bindings. "You couldn't erase *me*."

The threads tightened, holding him in place.

"I will go to Eira," he whispered, gritting his teeth. "She is mine." The sound of her name broke the silence like a stone shattering glass.

The Loom hesitated until the bindings loosened an infinitesimal amount. *"You would destroy the world for her?"*

"I would destroy the world for the *choice* to be with her," Adrian said firmly, golden light spilling between the threads that held him. "For the right to love without asking permission."

"If you cling to her," the voice said, caressing his thoughts, *"you will risk everything. All will burn."*

"Then let it burn. Let us all feel the consequences of suppressing free will," Adrian said, and meant every word.

Lines of pure light snapped free and recoiled, like veins ripped from a beating heart. For a moment, the whole structure seemed to falter, and in the distance he saw Eira's realm, trembling and unbalanced; on the very edge of collapse.

Adrian reached for it instinctively, heart twisting as he saw her move gracefully within her realm. Her face gentled the fury blazing in his veins, calmed the storm that was rising. The threads between them blazed white-hot, pain searing through every nerve as he fought to touch the vision shimmering before him. Pain roared through him, but he did not stop. He HAD to get to her. She was his, and he was hers.

"You cannot touch her!" The Loom thundered.

"I already have. I have touched her here," Adrian said softly, placing a hand across his heart.

"Then you have chosen," The Loom said, the voice caressing his mind. *"You are their destruction. Your mere existence threatens the Sovereigns."*

The threads released him abruptly and Adrian inhaled sharply as he collapsed to his knees. The echo of The Loom's words rang throughout the infinite chamber.

"Things can change," Adrian said, staring at Eira's reflection.

"We have seen the end. We know what is coming and we will not warn you again," it hissed, many voices yet one.

Adrian raised his head, defiantly. "That is a problem we will deal with later."

The light surged, pulsing furiously, and then it vanished. Darkness swept over him, vast and eternal. The threads were still, dimmed to dull gold as he looked around, expecting to hear the voice again. He did not.

Adrian rose slowly and straightened his shoulders, every line of him blazing with golden light. The mortal softness he carried was gone; what remained was the poise of divinity tempered by grief and anger. He looked upward into the endless weave.

"I will find you," he said quietly, holding Eira's image in his mind. He had memorized the sadness in her eyes, the fracture in her realm, and he knew he would have to go to her.

"I will fix this."

SNEAK PEEK: THE MOURNER'S SONG- PROLOGUE

Before time had a name, there were the old gods that existed and ruled in chaos. They were wild and radiant, filled with the hunger of creation. They shaped worlds that burned too brightly, then watched them fall to ash, displeased with their creations. They breathed life into monstrous creatures and called it worship, never caring that the prayers became chains to the ones who spoke them. Only one of them saw what was coming. He was called The Architect. He had been the first breath of creation and he would be the last.

Where his kin built from desire and wild abandon, he built from design. The Architect measured what they made and found no Balance, no mercy, and no order in their endless making. And so their war began, a clashing of great power and wills, until they were unmade. The old gods fell screaming into The Chasm, the womb who birthed all things. Their light sank into silence, and The Architect sealed the void with a single vow: *There will be Balance.*

But even order cannot quiet loneliness. From The Architect's solitude and The Chasm's emptiness, something new began to stir. Light and darkness tangled together, forming eleven divine beings born not of passion but of purpose. They were called the Sovereigns, and each had a duty. Life. Death. Knowledge. Mercy. Revenge. Pleasure. Pain. Fury. Peace. Joy. Sorrow. They were not created as the old gods had been, for they were born of the First Breath and the Last Silence.

The Sovereigns were the pulse that kept the universe and all things within it in rhythm. To guide them, The Architect wrote the Code, binding them to Balance. To guard the Code, he created The Fates; three eternal sisters who tended the Loom, the living tapestry of all that ever was, is, and will be. The Loom lived in a realm beyond time, its threads shimmering with the light of every life. When a thread's song ended, The Fates cut it. When the pattern faltered, they mended it. Their duty was to the loom and they tended to it faithfully.

For an age, all was still. Mortals lived and died as they were meant to. The Sovereigns watched and guided the mortal world as was their purpose as unseen, dutiful guardians. But silence can be dangerous, and perfection grows restless. In the stillness between worlds, the Sovereigns began to feel. Not duty, not purpose, simply *feeling* because it was not in their nature. Curiosity first. Then longing. Then love.

When The Architect noticed this disruption, watching from the silence between stars, he whispered to The Fates, *"If the children of Balance forget why they were born, let the Loom teach them."*

And it did.

ACKNOWLEDGEMENT

Thank you for reading *Threads of Fate!* I hope you've come to love these characters as much as I do. There's a bit of Sovereign in all of us! Sometimes we're Peace, sometimes Fury, sometimes Sorrow or Mercy. The trick is to keep moving forward, even when the world feels against you.

To all my Sovereigns out there — thank you for walking this path with me. I hope you're ready for what's coming next.

About the Author

Lana has loved writing since childhood, starting with poetry and growing into full-length stories. A lifelong reader, she gravitates toward fantasy, science fiction, and romance, especially the spicy kind! She has always enjoyed reading and writing fantasy because it lets her dream without limits, create magic, and share that wonder with readers. These genres continue to inspire her storytelling, and she loves building worlds filled with magic, emotion and high stakes. When she isn't writing, Lana enjoys traveling, tending to her plants, and spending time outdoors, where she finds both creativity and calm.

https://www.lanajwilliams.com
facebook.com/LanaJWilliamsAuthor
goodreads.com/thereallanajauthor
tiktok.com/@thereallanajauthor

ALSO BY LANA J. WILLIAMS

THE MOURNER'S SONG: CHRONICLES OF THE SOVEREIGNS (BOOK 2)

A Sovereign of Death, bound by unyielding devotion, resists a temptation that could unravel eternity.

A Sovereign of Sorrow dares to break the oldest law and love a mortal, only to learn that fate does not bend for desire.

A Sovereign of Pleasure tempts mortals with delights that always demand their price.

The lesson is eternal: fate always demands balance.

The Mourner's Song is the prequel to the *Chronicles of the Sovereigns* saga, *Threads of Fate,* a sweeping romantasy of desire, defiance, and divine consequence.

Stay updated by signing up to receive emails at www.lanajwilliams.com.